GW00870460

CHRISTMAS PRESENCE

LISA HOBMAN

This is a fictional work. The names, characters, incidents, places, and locations are solely the concepts and products of the author's imagination or are used to create a fictitious story and should not be construed as real. Any similarities of characters to persons alive or dead is purely coincidental and should therefore not be construed as real.

Christmas Presence
Lisa Hobman
Copyright Lisa Hobman 2014/2017
First Published by 5 Prince Publishing 2014
Second Edition Published by Lisa Hobman 2017

Cover The Graphics Shed

All rights reserved. No part of this book may be used or reproduced in any manner whatsoever without written permission, except in the case of brief quotations, reviews, and articles. For any other permission please contact Lisa Hobman at http://facebook.com/LisaJHobmanAuthor

First Printing November 2014Printed U.S.A.
Second Edition Printing 2017 Printed UK

For Rich and Gee. You make every day feel like Christmas.

CONTENTS

Mallory stared out at the Atlantic Ocean from her favourite spot on the bridge. The winter sun glistened on the surface of the water, and she squinted as she watched Greg crouch, one hand still on the pram where baby Sylvie sat, to show little Mairi something on the ground. She guessed it was a bug or a pretty stone like usual. He was such a good daddy. Ever keen to show their daughters the simple wonders of the world. Mairi giggled, the joyous sound travelling on the breeze to warm Mallory's heart. There was nothing else in the world that she needed. Greg and her girls were all the Christmas gifts she could ever wish for.

As if he felt her eyes on him, Greg glanced up and waved to her. His mouth tilted up at one side in that panties-melting way that made her toes curl. She returned his smile. The butterflies took flight inside her as they often did when she looked at him. He never ceased to affect her that way. He really was gorgeous. Raising her hand, she waved back. His shaggy, dark hair was swept back from his face but flopped forward as he leaned toward the ground. His winter jacket hid the bulk of his biceps—one of her favourite parts of his body.

It was yet another uncharacteristically warm December morning, and the view from the bridge was as stunning as ever. She turned her head, and her gaze settled on the pub where so much of her new life now centred, and she smiled again. Home. She was home. Stella waved from the benches where she cleared Ron's empty glass from the table. From there Mallory turned again and took in the scene over at the shop where Colin and Christine unloaded packages from the trunk of their car, rolls of brightly coloured paper peeking out from several bags. They must've been Christmas shopping. She loved these people like family. Since losing her own parents, she had forgotten what it was like to be cared for so deeply, but these people took her in and made her one of them. One of their own. The village of Clachan-Seil and her beloved bridge were so very special to her now that she could not imagine being anywhere else. The proud Scots pine tree in the parking area danced in the breeze, its branches adorned with red, green, and gold ornaments, and Mallory could smell its fresh, Christmassy scent.

When she turned to look back to where Greg and their girls were, the empty pram was standing abandoned.

Her heart stuttered in her chest. Suddenly filled with panic, she gasped and set off running to where she'd last seen her husband and children.

"Greg! Greg!" she tried to call out, but her voice was nothing more than a strangled whisper as it left her throat. Her heart pounded and a sheen of sweat broke out on her skin. *He must be in the house. It's fine. He'll just be in the house.* She struggled up the path to their front door, her feet growing heavier with each step. She peered down at her leaden legs, suddenly feeling like she was walking through quicksand. Looking up again, she found the door wide open. Panic rose anew within her. She tried to call out, but there was no reply to her whispered attempts.

After dashing through the cottage and checking every room, she stumbled, sobbing, back toward the bridge and across to the pub. Yanking the door open, she stepped inside to find the place deserted. *What the hell?* It was like a scene from some scary movie in which everyone had disappeared into thin air. She spun around, searching each dark corner, her heart hammering as if trying to escape the cage of her ribs. Dizziness overtook her, but she clambered forward, stumbling as fabric began to tangle around her legs. Music began to play as if out of nowhere... She thrashed, trying to discover the source of the song, but suddenly felt paralysed. *What's going on?* The familiar music got louder and louder...

CHAPTER 1

Mallory's eyes fluttered open as the noise to her left registered in her fuzzy, sleep-fogged brain as the song "I Predict a Riot". Confusion niggled at her mind as she realised she was in bed. Her *own* bed in her *own* room. Greg moaned beside her and rolled over, trapping her under his muscular, tattooed arm and nuzzling her neck. The quick pounding of her heart began to calm as delicious tingles awoke on her skin where Greg's breath had settled. It had been just a dream. A sense of relief replaced the rush of adrenaline, and she smiled as she snuggled closer to her man. Glancing at the illuminated display on her clock, she squinted at the numbers. *Five o'clock? Urgh... too early.*

"Are you going to answer that, Mally? It's a bit too early for the Kaiser Chiefs, don't you think?" he mumbled into her skin, ending his sentence with a kiss. A shiver traversed her body, making her sigh in contentment. *Ahhh! Ringtone... that explains it. Oh shit, Brad's ringtone.*

She grappled with Greg's heavy arm and pushed it off her body. Stretching out her arm, she reached for her phone. "Hello?" she said as a feeling of panic washed over her and her heart began to race.

"Mal, oh, thank God. It's started. It's early!" a very worried voice gasped down the line.

She sat bolt upright. "Oh, no, Brad! Is she okay?"

"She's terrified. They've said... there are... there are complications. We're at the General right now. I'm really sorry, but Le Petit Cadeau will have to stay closed today."

"Brad, I couldn't care less about the shop, all I'm worried about is Josie and the baby. She shouldn't have been working this late into her pregnancy anyway. This isn't the best way for things to go."

"I know. I know. Shit, Mal, what if things go wrong and—" Brad's voice broke and a lump lodged in Mallory's throat.

She made a concerted effort to sound calm. "Stop it right now. *Nothing* is going to go wrong, Brad. So this is all happening a month early. So what? Hospitals are well equipped to deal with these situations nowadays. You've got to stay positive. Do you hear me? For Josie."

Greg sat up and put his arm around her, taking her free hand in his, a frown etched on his rugged features. She stroked the back of his hand with her thumb, turned to face him, and shook her head, hoping he would understand the seriousness of the situation. He closed his eyes and dropped his head forward, squeezing her into his firm chest and kissing the top of her head. With the phone still pressed to her ear, she was grateful to be in Greg's strong and warm embrace. Memories of the loss she had felt in her dream came flooding back, and she bit down on her lip in a bid to abate the threatening tears. Brad must be experiencing similar fears right now and she wanted—no, needed —to help.

Brad sniffed down the line, making Mallory's heart ache. "You're right, I'm sorry... I just... I don't know what I'd do..."

"Look, I'm going to come down. I'll... I'll sort it so that I can come down today." Greg pulled away, nodded his agreement beside her and kissed her shoulder.

Brad huffed out a breath. "No, don't do that. The roads are terrible up there right now. We saw it on the news last night. Honestly, please don't, we'll be fine."

"Brad, you're my best friends. You *need* me. I'll get a train. And I won't take no for an answer, so don't bother trying to argue."

"But... it's a week until Christmas, Mal. Greg and the girls need you to be there."

"And I *will* be. I'll come down for a few days, and I'll be back here in plenty of time for Christmas. Don't worry."

Brad heaved a long, shaking breath. "Well, I have to admit, having you here would be good. You have such a calming effect on Josie. And me, for that matter. And knowing you've been through all of this... *twice*... it's... reassuring. Look... I should go. I need to get back to my girl."

"That's that, then. I'll text when I get a ticket sorted so you know what time to expect me." She said her goodbyes and set the phone on the night-stand. But when she turned back to Greg, her lip began to quiver as tears welled in her stinging eyes. "Something's wrong, Greg. She's gone into early labour, and they've said there are complications." A sob broke free from her throat as he pulled her into his arms.

"Oh, shit, sweetheart. You should go. You're

right. Me and the girls will be fine. She needs you right now."

Pulling away, she looked into his chocolate-brown eyes and saw such understanding. *Could this man be any more perfect?* "Thank you. I know it's so close to Christmas and—"

"Hey, stop. Like I've said. We'll be fine. Go and be with our friends." He touched her face tenderly and then stood. She trailed her gaze down his sculpted, naked form. She would never tire of his masculinity. She watched as he pulled his lounge pants up the length of his muscular thighs, and when her gaze met his, he smiled knowingly. "I'll go and stick the kettle on whilst you have a look online for a ticket, okay?" He reached over, grabbed the tablet from his nightstand, and handed it to her.

Suddenly, excited high-pitched squealing could be heard along with the pitter-patter of little feet. "Mummy, Daddy! Santa!"

Mallory wiped at her eyes and turned toward her daughter. "Good morning, princess. I'm sorry, but Santa hasn't been yet. It's a little early. He doesn't come until next week." Little Mairi jumped onto Mallory's lap, her brown curls bouncing. Mallory cuddled her daughter and planted a kiss on her head. Mairi yawned and stuck her thumb in her mouth.

Giving her a squeeze, Mallory told her, "I think maybe you need to go back to bed for a little while. It's *very* early. Sylvie's still sleeping, and so should you be." She scooped up the little bundle and carried her back to the girlie pink bedroom along the landing and placed her back under her duvet. Mairi rolled over, grabbed her teddy, and closed her eyes.

Mallory walked over to the cot in the corner of the room. She gazed down at the baby girl sleeping soundly. A mop of dark hair spiked up from every angle. She kissed her finger and stroked it down her baby's cheek.

Sylvie had been a little surprise that had arrived when Mairi was only eighteen months old. It had been a huge shock for Mallory, discovering that she was pregnant again so soon after giving birth to her first daughter. Greg, however, had been like a child on Christmas morning all over again. His enthusiasm had been contagious and shock had soon become excitement for the happy couple. And now that he had a house full of girls, he and Angus—the yellow Labrador—were outnumbered four to two when Ruby the little black Patterdale was included, which, of course, she was.

Making her way back to the bedroom she shared with her husband, Mallory revived the sleeping tablet and located the rail website, where she searched for the next available train from Oban to Leeds. She would have a couple of hours to shower, get ready, and travel to the station. Plenty of time under normal circumstances, but the roads were treacherous at the moment after the latest heavy snowfall. She glanced out the bedroom window over the front garden. A blanket of white covered everything except for the Atlantic Ocean where it flowed in its icy glory just a few hundred yards in front of the little cottage. Glancing up to the right, she smiled as her gaze settled on the pretty arched bridge. Flakes of snow had gathered in the dents and striations of the stonework, creating a vista worthy of any Christmas card.

The bridge over the Atlantic had been the location of so many memories for her; some wonderful and some still painful. But her heart had no intention of allowing her to live elsewhere. She was still drawn to the place after all these years, and no matter how long she was away from it—whether a week, a weekend, or just a day—she still felt the pangs of homesickness. The sense of relief when returning home and crossing the bridge toward the cottage still resonated deep within her.

As she stood watching a fresh batch of

snowflakes flutter to the ground, Greg walked into the room. She turned to face him as he carefully carried two steaming mugs, a look of concentration on his face. The aroma of freshly brewed coffee accompanied him.

"There ya go, gorgeous. That should help clear away the wee cobwebs," he said as he held the mug toward her. His broad Scottish accent still made her tingle.

She smiled. "Thanks. I'm all sorted. The train leaves at eight. Do you think you could drive me to Oban if we ask Christine to look after the girls?" Driving in adverse weather conditions had terrified her since losing Sam, and Greg was far more experienced at driving than she was.

He crossed the room, placed his cup on the nightstand, and took her face in his palms. "I wouldn't have it any other way. I don't want you driving in this weather. You're too precious. And the Landy will cope with the roads now that the snow tyres are fitted." He leaned in and kissed her lips gently and she melted into him. He pulled away and tapped her nose with his finger. "Now you drink your coffee, get showered, and I'll go light a fire. I'll give Chrissy a call and see if she'll come over ASAP." He gazed down at her, a combination of adoration and worry in his eyes. "It'll all be fine, you know. I can just... feel it."

"I hope you're right," she replied with a wavering voice. Knowing that Josie had suffered a previous miscarriage and how that had affected her friends so deeply played on her mind. They'd been through enough already. She wasn't sure how they would get through this if it happened at such a late stage in the pregnancy.

CHAPTER 2

Once she was ready, Mallory made her way downstairs. The heat from the fire had already warmed the early morning air, and Greg had switched on the tree lights, giving the room a warm and cosy glow. Christmastime always reminded her of the day she'd first viewed the house with Sam. It seemed like an eternity ago, but the memory was still fresh in her mind.

"Okay, imagine this..." She walked over to the fireplace. "The log burner is crackling away with a fresh pine log... there's an evergreen-and-berry garland stretched across the mantel..." She gestured wildly to where the adornment would sit, and then she skipped to the corner of the room. "Over in this corner is a real Christmas tree, not one of those plastic artificial things..." She scrunched her nose at the

thought. "*No, a real tree trimmed with baubles and beads, filling the air with its fresh scent.*" *Glancing over to where Sam stood in the centre of the room, she crouched.* "*Under the tree are little brightly coloured packages, tied up with ribbons, waiting to be opened...*" *She rose again and sauntered back over to the fireplace and waved her hands at the empty floor space.* "*There's a rug in front of the fire and Ruby is curled up fast asleep...*" *Crouching again, she reached out her hand.* "*Eventually there will be a mini Sam or Mallory sitting wide-eyed, waiting for Santa to come... although explaining how he'll get through a stove may be tricky.*" *She laughed as she imagined that scenario. Standing again, she danced over toward the door that led through to the kitchen and closed her eyes.* "*There's a delicious aroma of spiced fruitcake floating through the house*"—*her fingers flickered around in the air*—"*and in the background Bing Crosby is singing about snow.*" *She brought her arms around her body and sighed. Breaking herself from her vision, she turned to Sam.* "*Hey, are you okay, honey?*" *His eyes had misted over.*

Sam had been the man who had given her the confidence to accept her curves. He had loved her *because* of them and not *despite* them. He had loved her unconditionally, and losing him on the day they were supposed to start their new life together in the Highlands had broken her heart almost beyond repair. But Greg had helped her to mend and had filled her heart and her life with such love and the same acceptance that Sam had. She could regret losing Sam, but she could never regret the life he'd led her to.

Her guardian angel.

Walking into the living room, she smiled as she looked at the Christmas tree standing exactly where she had pictured it on that fateful day. The white lights twinkled and the smell of fresh pine infiltrated her senses. She closed her eyes and breathed deeply. An arm came about her as a melancholy mix of emotions washed over her.

"Hey... are you okay, sweetheart?" Greg asked, a concerned edge to his voice.

"Yes... yes, I'm fine. Just a little reminiscent, I think. This time of year always makes me look back when I should be looking forward."

He leaned and kissed her head. "Nothing wrong with remembering. Sam would've loved this place."

She opened her eyes and gazed up at him. "Don't you ever feel like you're living with his ghost?"

He frowned for a moment and then smiled warmly. "Well if his ghost *is* here, he's not unhappy. I

LISA HOBMAN

never feel uneasy or like he's angry with us for being in love. Do you?"

She pondered the question for a few seconds. "Not at all. He would've been happy that I found you. That we found each other."

"Well, there you go. Now stop with the worrying, Mrs McBradden, and let me make you some breakfast."

"Oh, thanks, but I'm not hungry yet. I'll grab something on the train."

The doorbell chimed and Greg huffed. "Make sure you do. The last thing I need is you starving yourself through worry. It won't do you any good."

She rolled her eyes as he made his way to the door. "Yes, boss," she chuntered.

"Heard that," he called from the small hallway. He greeted their friend Christine, who owned the shop in the village with her husband, Colin. An ice-cold breeze followed them back into the room.

"Goodness me, Mallory, you need to wrap up warm, dear. It's freezing out there." She hugged Mallory and held her at arm's length. "You go and don't worry about a thing here. Colin and I will be around for the girls when Greg goes to work. We'll all be fine. Just hurry back and stay safe, okay?"

"I'll do my best, Chrissy, thank you. And I really appreciate you coming over at such short notice."

"Not at all. That's what friends are for. Now, are you all packed and ready?"

"I am. I just need to grab my coat and we'll be off."

"I'll go and warm the Landy up a wee bit," Greg told her as he pulled on his thick coat and scarf.

Christine squeezed Mallory's arms and a look of sympathy took over her face. "I hope Josie and the baby are okay, dear. Such a shame that things have gone this way for them."

"I know. Me too. I'm trying so hard not to worry, but the more I dwell on it, the more I do. I'll let you know how things go." A deep-seated worry niggled at her mind that she would fall to pieces if the worst were to happen and she lost her best friend the way she had lost Sam, her parents, and her aunt Sylvia. The thought startled her and she shook her head to eradicate the negativity.

Christine pulled her in and wrapped her arms around her. "Please do. Now give me a big hug. I'll be thinking of you." Mallory's eyes began to sting and she fought back the threatening tears.

Greg appeared in the doorway again. "Come on, sweetheart, we should go."

"Okay, I'll just go say goodbye to the babies." Mallory hurried to the stairs.

Once in the girls' pink bedroom, she leaned to kiss her sleeping children. The last thing she wanted was to be away from them, especially so close to Christmas. But Josie needed her right now, and this pregnancy had been so tough. So many issues and hospital visits. And now... *complications*. It could mean so many things. Mallory missed her terribly, and living so far away when her best friend was suffering was very difficult. Taking one last look at her babies, she wiped her eyes and left the room, closing the door gently behind her.

CHAPTER 3

Mallory and Greg sat silently in the Landy for a while as Bing Crosby sang "White Christmas" whilst they negotiated the icy road toward Oban. The grey sky above was heavy with an imminent snowfall, and the heater was on the highest setting—but the scant heat being blown from the 1960s technology did little to warm Mallory's icy fingers. Greg's adoration for the rugged vehicle—and the grin on his face whenever he sat behind the wheel—made her smile. When she shivered, he leaned over, clutching her hand in his.

"You're very quiet, Mally. I'm worried about you. You seem... I don't know... down."

She turned to face him. "I'm okay. Just so worried about Josie. And about leaving you and the girls."

"It's only for a few days, darlin'. Try not to fret, eh? We'll be fine. I promise you that." He squeezed her hand. Oh, that accent. He could still turn her into a jellified puddle just by saying her name. She leaned her head to rest on the seat but kept her eyes fixed on his stubbled face. His dark, almost black hair swept back from his forehead in thick strands. His jawline, although covered partly by his beard, was strong and angular. His lips full and oh so kissable. She would miss those lips whilst she was away.

He glanced sideways at her and chuckled. "Liking the view, Mrs McBradden?"

"Always, Mr McBradden," she replied with a smile.

"I have to say, I'm going to miss waking up with your naked body wrapped around me." He released her hand and ran his fingers up and down her thigh. "I hate it when we're apart."

"Me too." Being away was something she avoided at all costs, but it was necessary every so often when she had to travel to Yorkshire to meet with Josie and talk business and marketing strategies for Le Petit Cadeau. The little craft shop had been thriving lately, and her second shop near home at Easdale had taken off well too, affording her an employee. But no matter how perfect her business and her marriage and family were, the nightmares about losing Greg like she'd lost Sam plagued her and clouded her mind through her waking hours. She was very much aware of the distance she was beginning to create between them and felt helpless to stop it.

Greg suddenly pulled the Landy to the side of the road. Mallory watched with confusion as he clenched and unclenched his jaw. After applying the handbrake, he turned in his seat to face her. "Are we okay, Mally? I mean... Are you starting to regret being with me?"

Guilt washed over her and she pulled her brows in. "Whatever has given you that idea?" She knew the answer full well.

He huffed out a long breath and dragged his hand through his hair. "I don't know... you've been a little... distant. I keep catching you staring at the bridge... or... or staring at the Christmas tree with that wistful look in your eyes. I know you're thinking about Sam. And that's understandable. But... now you're heading back to where it all started with him and I think... I think... I'm scared of losing you." His voice cracked along with her heart as she heard his admission. A crease appeared between his eyebrows, and his facial muscles ticked as he clenched and unclenched his jaw. He suddenly appeared younger and a little lost. Bereft, even. The sadness she saw in his eyes was almost palpable and she knew she was the cause.

Her stomach tightened into a knot and dropped as if she were on a roller coaster's steep descent. She was unintentionally breaking his heart, and after all he had done for her, he didn't deserve it. But knowing that didn't help the gnawing fear inside her to dissipate at all. She lost people. It's what always seemed to happen. How long would it be before she was alone again?

Realising she had been staring silently at his pained expression, she leaned forward and placed her chilled hands on his face. The heat from his skin warmed her. "Greg, you're *not* losing me. You'll *never* lose me. I've been back to Yorkshire many times and you've never reacted like this before." She was terrified that *she* would lose *him*, but the words of explanation wouldn't come.

He closed his eyes briefly and then seared her with his penetrating gaze. "I know... it's just that this time feels different somehow. I... I can't explain it."

"Look, I'm just worried about Josie right now." It was partly true. "And this time of year does make me think of Sam. But not in a way that means I regret being with *you*. That will *never* happen. You and me... we're forever, Greg. Okay?"

His nostrils flared and he closed his eyes once more. Leaning toward her, he covered her mouth with his and stole her breath in a passionate kiss, filled with love and desire. Her core clenched and she wished they were back in their king-sized bed, naked, where she could show him just how much he meant to her.

When the kiss ended, he pulled away and gazed into her eyes. "I love you so much," he whispered with fervour.

She smoothed her thumbs over his cheeks. "And I love you too."

As if satisfied with her answers, he turned and released the handbrake, pulling them onto the icy road once again.

After around forty minutes, they arrived at Oban station and Greg helped her out of the Landy. He lifted her wheeled case down from the car and they walked toward the station. McCaig's tower was visible up on Battery Hill, its black granite arches a stark silhouette against the grey winter sky.

The station was fairly quiet, and Greg hugged Mallory to him as they waited for the arrival of the train that would take her hundreds of miles away.

She buried her head into the juncture of his neck and shoulder and inhaled the natural, masculine scent of him. Eventually the train arrived at the platform and she pulled away from him. He cradled her chin with his free hand and tilted her face up. After gazing hungrily into her eyes, he leaned in to kiss her again. She clung to his jacket and kissed him back with every ounce of the passion she felt for him in the hope that she could put his doubts to rest.

She pulled away again and fought the tears that needled at her eyes. "Take care of my babies."

"And you take care of *you*." He clenched his jaw. She could still see the remnants of fear in his eyes and didn't know what to do to make him feel better.

She swept his hair back from his face. "I'll miss you. I can't wait until we can hold each other again."

He swallowed hard and bit the inside of his cheek. What on earth was going through his mind? She hated to know he was feeling so insecure. But what made it worse was knowing she'd had a hand in making him feel that way. She touched his cheek again and turned to board the train. The final whistle blew and the train began to pull away. She quickly found a seat and sat down. Leaning to face him where he stood on the platform, she placed her palm on the window and watched him through the glass as he disappeared from view.

Taking a deep breath, she texted him to tell him once again how much she loved him, and she resolved to spend her time confirming that in an intimate way when she returned home in a few days. After putting her phone back in her bag, she pulled out a magazine and turned the pages until she found the article about the artist Flick MacDuff and her latest exhibition in Edinburgh. She smiled as she admired the images of Flick's work which adorned the pages. Such a talent. The pieces that she painted from memory evoked such emotion in Mallory, and the places depicted made her homesick already—and she had been on the train only a few minutes. A text came through from Brad, indicating Josie was still in labour. It would be a long journey, that's for sure.

CHAPTER 4

After almost nine hours and two changes, Mallory's train pulled into Leeds station. The dimming light of the winter's day cast an ethereal glow over the bustling city she had once called home, rendering it almost unrecognisable. The tower blocks and office complexes in the city centre reached skyward as if trying to catch the final, diminishing UV rays as the sun made its descent. People stood on the platform, heads down, playing with their gadgets whilst they waited to make their journeys home from work. There was something incredibly impersonal about the place now, compared to home where everyone knew everything about one another. Homesickness suddenly washed over her as the sky darkened with an imminent rainfall. Tears for the ending day perhaps. The change in the weather seemed to match her mood.

She walked along the platform and exited the bustling station, dodging people laden down with brightly coloured bags emblazoned with red, green, and gold festive symbols. She narrowly missed being poleaxed by a tall man wielding a humongous roll of holly-covered wrapping paper like a Weedwacker. Chuntering, she managed to sidestep him and into the path of a group of giggling women in office attire —who already seemed a little worse for wear alcohol-wise. They zigzagged a path in front of her, singing "Merry Christmas Everybody" at passers-by. All of them were wearing ridiculous festive headgear, from reindeer antlers to candy cane deely boppers that bobbed around as they jigged left and right. Under normal circumstances the group would have brought a grin to Mallory's face as she told herself they'd regret it in the morning. But today she felt annoyed that the world was still gearing up for the Christmas season all around her, when inside she was feeling anything but festive.

She was completely exhausted. The last she had heard from Brad was that the midwife and obstetrician had been trying to bring the contractions to a halt, but things were not going according to plan.

She had texted to let him know she had arrived at the station and that she would get a taxi to the hospital, but she'd had no reply. Worry clouded her tired mind, and several emotions vied for the surface all at once. After flagging down a cab, she climbed in and gave the driver her destination. Once she had fastened her seat belt, she dialled Greg's number.

He answered on the first ring. "Hey, sweetheart. Are you okay?"

"Hi. Yes, I'm fine. Just tired. I'm on my way to the hospital. Are you and the girls okay?"

"We're... we're fine. We had a few tears when Mairi realised you were gone, and Sylvie must be sensing it too as she's been restless today."

"Oh no. My poor girls." Her voice wavered as her heart sank.

Greg sighed. "I shouldn't have said anything. I didn't mean to upset you, darlin'. Don't worry. They just miss you. And... so do I." He sounded so despondent.

She tried to keep her tone light. "It's not for long. I'll be home before you know it."

"I know. Give my love to Josie and her ugly spud of a husband for me."

She smiled. She knew he was trying to lift the

mood too. "I will. Give my girls a hug and kiss from Mummy."

"Of course. Keep me posted, okay? Love you."

"Love you too." She ended the call. The cab pulled up outside the General and Mallory paid the driver. Once she had unloaded her case, she made her way inside.

On arrival at the maternity wing, she was pulled into huge muscular arms by Brad, who sobbed into her hair. "Fuck, Mal, I'm so glad to see you. They've taken her into theatre. She's been in there so long. I'm terrified I'll lose them both."

She barely held up the towering man as he crumpled in her arms. "Hey, shhh. They'll both be fine. You have to believe that. You have to stay positive." She wished she could believe her own words, but the fact that Josie was in surgery filled her with dread. Stomach-churning, heartbreaking, nausea-inducing dread.

After leading Brad into the family room, she sat beside him where he almost collapsed into a chair. In the corner of the room stood a small, artificial Christmas tree—the kind Mallory hated. The brightly coloured decorations and multicoloured lights adorning the branches were completely at odds with the harrowing situation the friends found themselves in, and she had the urge to throw something at it. How could the world be so excited about the festive season when her best friend was suffering?

Brad sniffed loudly. "They're performing an emergency C-section. The baby..." He sobbed again. "The baby was distressed, and its heart rate was getting weak. I've never seen Jose in so much pain, Mal. I couldn't do anything. I feel so utterly fucking useless." He leaned forward and rested his head in his hands, and more sobs racked his huge body. Seeing this strong man in such a distraught state made tears escape her eyes. She gripped his hand and held on tight.

He squeezed his eyes closed. "If I lose her... I'll... I'll die, Mal. I can't live without her."

She clenched her teeth as determination overtook anguish. "No! I won't listen to you talk like that. If you lost her, Brad—and it's a big *if*, because the doctors won't let that happen—but if it did, you would go on. You'd have to go on. You'd have a little baby to care for. And so you'd have to be strong. Do you hear me? But she's not going anywhere. She's going to be fine. Are you listening to me?"

Brad raised his head. His bloodshot, damp eyes searched hers as if trying to figure out if he could believe her. "Do you really think so?"

"I *know* so." *Because I went on after I lost Sam.* "Josie is a tough girl. She's always been there for me, and I'm not about to let her go now. So stop it with the negativity."

He nodded and wiped his eyes and nose on his sleeve. "Yeah... she's a tough bird. She won't leave me."

She forced a smile. "That's more like it."

The door to the family room opened, and a man in green scrubs entered. "Mr Farnham?"

Brad stood and wiped his palms down his jeans. He cleared his throat. "Is she okay?"

"Mr Farnham, please take a seat." The doctor gestured to the chair Brad had just vacated.

Brad pulled his shoulders back and straightened up. "No... just tell me. Please."

Mallory's heart pounded in her chest. Why was the doctor insisting that Brad sit? What had happened?

"Mrs Farnham has lost a lot of blood. She's sleeping. We'll know more in a few hours."

The colour seeped from Brad's face, and the doctor reached to steady his shoulder for a moment. Brad nodded. "And... and the baby?"

The doctor smiled. "Your son is small, Mr Farnham. But he's a fighter. He's in the special care baby unit right now."

Brad collapsed into the chair and burst into floods of tears. "Will he... will he be okay?"

"We certainly hope so. He needs a little help breathing at the moment, but that's normal with a premature birth. I know it's easier said than done, but please try not to worry. He's getting the best care possible. You can see him if you like. Just head along to the SCBU when you're ready. We'll keep you posted about your wife and let you see her as soon as possible. And congratulations." The doctor shook Brad's hand and then left the room, closing the door gently behind him.

Brad lifted his head and turned to Mallory. Tears spilled from his red-rimmed eyes. "I'm... I'm a daddy, Mal."

Allowing tears to fall unabashedly down her own cheeks, Mallory nodded with a smile. "You certainly are, Brad. Shall we go and see your son?" She stood and held out her hand. Brad grasped it and let her pull him to his feet.

After following the signs to the special care baby unit, they informed the nurse at the desk that they were there to see Baby Farnham. She smiled warmly and led the way to the room where the baby was being cared for. Once they had washed their hands and applied sanitiser, they were allowed entry into the room.

Baby Farnham lay in an incubator. A CPAP breathing apparatus covered most of his face. He was tiny but he had all his fingers and toes and was so very beautiful. Mallory's gaze shifted to the card showing the baby's details. Her throat tightened as she read the weight. Two pounds and twelve ounces. Not much bigger than a bag of sugar. How would he survive in the world when he wasn't meant to be here for another two months?

Brad gasped and sat on the chair placed beside the crib for him by the nurse.

He placed his palm flat on the transparent casing and spoke in a soft voice. "Hey, little man... I'm your daddy. I love you so much. Your mummy will come and see you as soon as she's feeling better. But she loves you too. She's been so excited about meeting you. We both have. You've arrived a bit earlier than we expected, but... it's fine. I'm just glad you're fighting, little man. Keep fighting. Keep getting stronger so that your mummy and I can take you home. You're going to be spoiled rotten, you know." He glanced up at Mallory with a big, beaming smile on his face. "Isn't he beautiful, Mal?"

"He really is, Brad. Just gorgeous." Her heart clenched in her chest as tears left damp trails in their wake. Hearing him speak to his newborn son was the sweetest thing she'd heard since Greg had said similar words to Sylvie.

The door opened and another nurse appeared. "Mr Farnham. The doctor has asked me to come and tell you that you're okay to go see your wife now."

Without taking his eyes from his baby boy, Brad nodded. "Thank you. I'll be right there." The door closed once again.

CHAPTER 5

Legs shaking, Mallory walked with Brad as he made his way to visit Josie. Her heart hammered in her chest and fear gripped her insides, tying them in knots and making her feel nauseated. The thought of losing her best friend tormented her despite her efforts to push it from her mind. They arrived outside the room and were greeted by a nurse who winked at Mallory while confirming she was "immediate family" and thus a permitted visitor.

"One at a time, please. She's still unconscious, but do speak to her."

Brad looked apologetically at Mallory and reached out to squeeze her shoulder. She smiled reassuringly at him. "Go on. Go see the new mummy." He nodded and walked through the door.

Mallory sat down on a chair opposite Josie's

room, and as she leaned her head back, she closed her eyes. Images of the day of Josie and Brad's wedding played in her mind. They had married the previous Christmas...

Josie stood before the mirror in her fitted wedding dress, her petite frame covered in lace. Mallory's eyes welled with tears. "You look so beautiful, Josie."

Josie turned to face her best friend. "Thank you so much for coming. Especially when you've been so unwell this last week or so. I've been so worried that you wouldn't make it."

Mallory stepped toward her and took her hands. "I wouldn't miss your wedding day for the world. And... I'm fine... honestly," she lied.

Josie scrunched her face, clearly not buying the all-is-well front that Mallory was trying so hard to project. "Pull the other one, you daft bat. You forget how well I bloody know you. Now be honest. How are you feeling?"

"It's nothing... I'm... I'm fine." Mallory's lip quivered as she fought back the mixture of emotions bubbling to the surface.

Concern washed over Josie's features. "There's something you're not telling me. Out with it, Mally. You're scaring me."

Mallory dabbed at her eyes, angry with herself for

getting upset. "No... it can wait. Today is your special day, and I'm not going to hog it with my crap."

Josie pulled away from Mallory's grip and placed her hands on her hips. "Do you want me to get pissed off? Because you know I will. Now tell me what the feck is going on or I'll slap you."

Josie was, at first glance, the epitome of elegance and class. Her small stature and blonde hair, however, belied the tough girl underneath. She appeared so fragile and demure—until she opened her gob, and her strong Yorkshire accent came out with expletives that could turn the air blue. Mallory couldn't help the snorty laugh that escaped. "You're so lovely."

"Yeah, well, I'm about to turn green and rip my dress, so come on. Tell me what's wrong or I swear you won't like what happens next."

Mallory turned and walked to the other side of the plush hotel suite. She plopped herself into the large chocolate-brown armchair and dropped her head into her hands. "I'm pregnant."

There was an audible intake of breath. "Eh? What do you mean you're fecking pregnant?"

Mallory snapped her head up and glared at her best friend. "I mean there is another baby growing in my belly. What the hell do you think I mean?"

"But... but... you... Mairi... how?" Josie stuttered.

"Crikey, the future Mrs Farnham at a loss for words. I've seen it all now."

"Are you sure? Does Greg know? Are you happy? Is that why you've been puking so much? Are you keeping it? Are you sure?" The questions were fired as if being released from some kind of verbal machine gun.

"Bloody hell, Jose. Give me a chance to answer."

Josie held her hands up in surrender. "Sorry... sorry."

"Okay... Here goes... Yes, I'm very sure. I've been to the doctor's. Yes, Greg knows and is over the moon. No, I'm not exactly happy, seeing as my body has only just bloody recovered from the last infant that I squeezed out. Yes, that's why I've been puking so much. Yes, of course I'm bloody keeping it, and I can't believe you even asked that. And finally, once again, yes, I'm bloody sure!"

Josie crossed the room and dropped to her knees before Mallory. "Oh, Mally, love. How can you not be happy?"

Mallory widened her eyes. "Were you not listening when I mentioned my body and the recovery from the last melon-sized baby I pushed out of my vagina?"

Josie started to laugh. At first she was visibly

fighting it, but her shoulders shuddered, her lips contorted, and her eyes watered. Mallory stared in annoyance. She folded her arms over her chest. "I'm glad you find it funny. You're supposed to be my best bloody friend."

Josie guffawed for a while as Mallory watched the tears stream down her face. "I'm... I'm so sorry, honey. But... but the way you said vagina... hilarious! I'm sorry... I'm calm now... honestly."

Mallory pursed her lips as a smile tried its best to spread across her reluctant face. "It's okay. You're forgiven. It's your wedding day, after all. I... I didn't want to spoil things for you."

Josie frowned. "How the hell would you be spoiling my day? You've just given me the best wedding gift ever! Baby news always turns me into a pile of mush, as you know. Now give me a fecking hug, you daft cow. And stop getting all fecking worked up." She grappled Mallory into a bear hug. "You only have to look at that gorgeous little girl you have to know how wonderful this is. And think of it this way, the closer they are in age, the easier it'll be."

Mallory scrunched her face. "How the hell do you figure that out?"

Josie shrugged. "It gets all the crappy nappies out

of the way in one go. They grow up together and become the best of friends."

"Hmmm, or they despise each other and I have an all-out sibling war on my hands."

"Oh, Mally, you're such a fecking drama queen. You'll adore that little bundle when it arrives. You know you will."

"I know... I know. It's just a little scary. I'll get used to the idea... and what's all this 'fecking' business?"

"Well... it's not quite the same as swearing, and"—she gestured to Mallory's tummy—"you know... little ears listening and all that."

Mallory burst into fits of laughter at her crazy friend. "You do know that swearing in an Irish accent is still swearing, don't you?"

Josie's cheeks coloured bright red and she joined in with the laughter. "Oh, shit. I hadn't realised that's what it was! God, I'm so blonde!"

"Erm, Miss Gardiner, I think that's rather insulting to the blondes in the world who actually have two brain cells to rub together," Mallory teased.

Josie lightly slapped Mallory's arm. "Oy! Cheeky sod!"

There was a knock at the door. "Josie, darlin', are

you coming to get wed or what?" Greg's voice vibrated through the closed door.

"Be right there," Josie replied modestly.

The ceremony was taking place in a little church in the grounds of the country house hotel and had been limited to close family and friends on account of their limited funds. Greg was giving Josie away, and Brad's brother, Ant, was proudly taking the role of best man. The Landy had been decorated with ribbon and balloons, and when Mallory escorted her shaking best friend down to the hotel foyer, Greg, dressed in his kilt, held the rear door of the car open for them.

Josie gasped as they reached the shiny vehicle. "Shit, Greg, you've even washed the car!"

"Aye, of course I have. What kind of heathen do you take me for?" He glanced over at Mallory and winked. She giggled and felt the heat rise in her cheeks. He looked absolutely gorgeous, and she was sure her panties would melt right then and there.

Josie glanced between the two of them. "Good grief, you two. You're like a pair of bloody teenagers."

Without taking his eyes from Mallory's, he said, "That's because this woman makes me crazy with lust, and I love her with all my heart, Jose."

Josie covered her mouth and laughed as she made fake retching noises. "Get me a bucket, quick!"

The two friends climbed into the car, and Mallory smoothed her, holly-green satin dress. As the wedding was so close to Christmas, the colours chosen had been particularly festive. Josie's small hand-tied bouquet of Christmas roses and berries was interspersed with mistletoe, and she had commented that the bouquet would come in handy later. The suggestive eyebrow wiggle that had accompanied her words had made Mallory laugh out loud.

After driving the quarter of a mile within the grounds to get to the little church, Greg brought the car to a halt and climbed out. He helped the two women down from the vehicle. In ten steps they arrived at the door of the church, and Josie took in a deep, shaking breath.

Mallory turned to her friend. "Josie, you look beautiful. Brad is such a lucky man. The two of you have been destined for this day since high school, and I'm so happy to be a part of it. I love you both dearly. You're my family."

Josie's lip quivered. "Stop it, you'll make me cry. Thank you again for coming all this way. You're the best, best friend a girl could ask for."

Mallory smiled. "You're not so bad yourself. Now come on. Brad'll be panicking. You know what he's like."

Greg pushed open the ornately carved oak doors, and the opening bars of "You're Still the One" by Shania Twain began to play. He held out his elbow, and Josie linked her arm through his. After Mallory began to walk, Josie and Greg followed.

Glancing over her shoulder, Mallory could see Josie's eyes glistening with tears ready to spill over and Greg simply beaming, his eyes crinkled in that cute way they did when he smiled widely. He wore the expression of a proud father and she could imagine him giving their daughter, Mairi, away in the future. The thought brought a lump to her throat. Turning to face the altar once again, she focussed her attention on Brad. He had the biggest smile fixed in place on his handsome features. The love he felt for Josie was written all over his face. Happiness radiated from his very being, and Mallory's eyes began to sting once again.

CHAPTER 6

The door to Josie's hospital room opened. A rather drained Brad stepped out and sat beside Mallory.

"How is she doing?" she asked.

He huffed out a long breath. "Hard to say really. There are all sorts of machines attached to her, and she looks so pale. How would I cope without her, Mal?" His lip quivered.

"You can't keep thinking like that. You have to stay positive. You have a little boy to think of. He needs both of you."

Brad leaned forward and ran his hands through his greasy hair. "And *I* need *her*, Mal."

Anger began to rise within her. "And you still *have* her, Brad. You're talking like she's bloody dead or something. Stop it."

He shook his head. "I'm sorry. I'm just struggling to get my head around all of this. One minute she was wrapping Christmas gifts, and the next she was in agony. I felt so fucking useless, and I *still* feel fucking useless."

"Well, you're not useless. You're a new father who's worried about the well-being of his son and his wife. No man would cope well in that situation. Just... just do your best to stay strong. I'll do whatever I can for the next few days, and after Christmas I'll come back down if you need me."

Brad's smile was tinged with sadness. "Thanks, Mal. You're a great friend. The best, in fact. Now go on in and see her."

Mallory nodded and stood. She smoothed her skirt down and took a deep breath. *Come on, McBradden, you can do this. Practise what you preach. Be strong.* She walked through the door to the room and gasped. Josie was, as Brad had warned her, hooked up to monitors and drips. Her skin was pale and grey. Her eyes were closed, and the skin around them was sunken and dark. She had clearly been through the wringer.

Sadness washed over Mallory, and her stomach knotted. She walked over and sat beside her best friend, grasping her limp hand and stroking her thumb over her pallid skin. The smell of disinfectant assaulted her nostrils, bringing back memories of her own stays in hospital. Although hers had been somewhat happier occasions.

The continuous and regular bleeping of the heart monitor was a reassuring sign that all was as well as it could be under the circumstances. But Mallory found herself glancing over every couple of minutes just to make sure. She wanted nothing more than for Josie to wake and tell her off for being a soppy cow. Josie always told things as she saw them, and Mallory would've loved the banter right now.

"Hey, bestie... you gave us quite a scare. I'm... I can't believe that you're in here attached to machines when your beautiful little boy is waiting to meet you. You must get better soon, Josie. You *must*." Her voice broke and she clenched her eyes shut for a moment. Willing herself to be positive, she opened them. "When you're better, we're going to have a big celebration. You could bring your little family up to Scotland, and we can introduce your son to his future wife. Oh, Jose, can you imagine that? Sylvie and... oh, gosh, you have to wake up so you can name your son. Baby Farnham is a bit of a mouthful really." She sat in silence for a few moments. "Greg thinks I'm going off him. He's gotten all worried. I have no clue why. Well... that's not exactly true. I've been thinking about Sam a lot lately. Greg has seen me drifting off into my own little world, and he thinks I'm regretting being with him. I'm not. I adore Greg. Remember that time when you said that Sam was some kind of guardian angel who led me to Greg? Well... I think you were right. You're usually right. That's why I need you to get better. I need you in my life, Josie. And so does that gorgeous baby boy."

The door opened and a nurse walked in. "I'm sorry, but I'm going to have to ask you to leave now. We need to run some more tests."

Mallory stood. "Oh... right. Yes, of course. I'll come back tomorrow if that's okay?"

"Of course. We're hoping to see some improvements. I've just mentioned to Mr Farnham that we'll contact him if there are any changes."

"Thanks." She looked back to Josie. "I've got to go, honey. But I'll come back tomorrow. I think I'll go to the shop and open up for a few hours. It might do me good to be there again. And I know how much you'll panic if you find out it's been closed." She bent to kiss her friend's forehead. "See you soon, sweetie. Keep getting well. I love you." She squeezed Josie's hand, and with a heavy heart, left the room.

Back at Brad and Josie's house that night—the house she had once called home herself—Mallory lay in the guest room bed, unable to sleep. She could hear Brad moving around downstairs and was toying with the idea of going down and making them both a hot chocolate. But the house phone began to ring and she sat bolt upright. Brad had answered. She tried to hear what was being said, but he obviously was trying to stay quiet so as not to wake her. She grabbed her robe and pulled it on whilst making her way downstairs, panicking at why the phone would be ringing at this time of night.

As she got closer she could hear that Brad's voice was filled with joy. "Great, thank you. That's brilliant news. Thank you so much. I'll be right there." He ended the call just as Mallory walked into the living room. He swung around, and with a beaming smile and tears streaming down his face, he grasped her arms. "She's awake, Mal. She's awake."

Relief rushed throughout her body and she pulled him into a hug. "See, I knew she'd be fine. Are you going through to see her?"

He grinned. "Yup. Wild horses couldn't

stop me."

She clapped her hands together. "Fab! Give me five minutes and I'll come with you."

"Great. I'll go get dressed." He rushed out of the room and Mallory followed.

Ten minutes later and they were steadily driving along the icy Yorkshire roads in Brad's new family car that he'd insisted on buying when Josie had announced that she was pregnant. Snow had begun to fall in earnest, making driving conditions difficult. The journey to the hospital took longer than expected, and Brad was chomping at the bit when they arrived. Mallory had to almost run to keep up with him as he dashed down the corridors towards his wife's room.

Once they arrived at the nurses' station, Mallory was quite out of breath. Brad smiled widely at the nurse on duty. "Hi, I had a call to say that Josie, my wife, is awake."

"Yes, Mr Farnham. She's quite tired, but she woke up and was asking for you. I understand your need to see her, but I must ask that you keep the visit short. She's been through major surgery."

"I know, I get that, but I do need to see her. I'll not stay long."

The nurse smiled and motioned for him to go

into the side room which was situated just off the maternity ward. Mallory followed him in and stood back as he tiptoed toward the bed. Josie's eyes were closed. He bent to kiss her head. "Hi, babe. I'm here," he whispered as he stroked her hair.

Josie's eyes fluttered open. "Brad... Brad, honey. I'm shattered. Have you seen him?" she asked weakly, her speech slightly slower than normal.

"Our little boy? I have, and he's bloody gorgeous. I'm so proud of you." His purposefully quiet voice broke as she reached up to wipe a tear away.

"Hey, hey. I'm fine... Sore but fine. I can't wait to see him." Her eyes opened and closed sleepily.

"You'll fall for him immediately just like I did. But... the little guy needs a name, babe. We didn't even finish deciding when he showed up early."

"I know, poor little love. We'll have to decide quick. Can't introduce a nameless baby to your mum and dad, can we?"

Brad chuckled. "No, I don't suppose we can. Oh, and Mal's here."

Josie turned her head and squinted in the limited light. "Mally? You came all this way?"

Mallory stepped forward. "Of course I did. I wanted to make sure you were okay and meet my new nephew."

Josie held out her hand and Mallory grasped it. "Thank you for coming all this way. It's so lovely to see you, bestie."

Mallory leaned and hugged her friend carefully. "I'm so glad you're okay, Jose. We've both been so worried."

"Where's Greg... and... the girls?" she slurred.

"Oh, they're back home. He insisted he could cope and that I should come and be here for you."

"Bless him. Remind me to give him a hug when I see him. It's so good to know you guys are okay. Good grief, do I sound drunk or what?" She giggled. "Must be the morphine. I'll be seeing giant talking pink rabbits next." Her giggles subsided and were replaced by a puzzled expression. "I... I remember a dream I had."

Brad stroked Josie's hair. "You do? What was it about?"

Josie glanced up at him and then at Mallory. "Greg and Mally. Things were... You weren't... There was this man who looked... Oh, forget it. It was just a dream."

Mallory's heart palpitated. "Why, what happened in your dream?"

Josie shook her head. "Nothing. No it's fine. Just ignore me."

Mallory had never been one to believe in the meaning of dreams, but now that it came to her best friend dreaming about *her*, she was intrigued. And a little scared. "No, go on, Jose. What was the dream about?"

Josie sighed and shook her head. "You and Greg were... you were broken up. You'd... you'd *left* him. It was awful." A crease appeared in Josie's brow, and the limited colour she had drained from her face.

Mallory's eyes widened, but Brad shook his head and laughed nervously. "Well, we know that's not going to happen. They're solid. Aren't you, Mal?"

"We... we are, but..." Mallory immediately regretted saying anything. Josie certainly didn't need this right now.

Josie turned to face her, worry etched on her face. "What? You're what? Is everything okay?"

Mallory nodded and shrugged. "We're fine."

"Mally. You'll not leave me here stewing over it, so just tell me."

"It's fine, honestly. Anyway, I don't want to talk about me. I'm here for you, remember?"

"Mallory McBradden, I swear if you don't tell me, I'll find someone to clonk you one, seeing as I don't have the energy. Spit it out. Now. Or else."

She didn't deserve such a good friend. But it was

clear Josie wasn't going to drop the subject. She shook her head. "I've just been... a bit distant. I struggle with this time of year, that's all. I've just been thinking about Sam. Wondering what life would be like if he still were here."

Josie's brow scrunched and Brad's mouth fell open. "But why, honey? Why would you be thinking about all that? You adore Greg. And you have the girls. I don't understand."

"No, me neither. And I *do* love Greg. I *adore* him. We're so happy. It's not that I don't want to be with him. I just keep daydreaming about Sam and how I lost him for some reason, and it's getting to Greg. But... the truth is... the truth is, I'm scared I'm going to lose *him* like I lost Sam." Mallory swallowed past the lump in her throat and inhaled a deep breath.

Brad squeezed her shoulder. "Oh, Mally. Why would you think that?"

"I don't know. I nearly lost him once... in the boat accident. And... I feel like I'm pulling away from him to... I don't know... protect myself."

"That's crazy, Mal. You two have been through *so much*. You're meant to be together," Brad insisted.

"I believe that we are. Don't get me wrong. But... seeing you in here... worrying over Josie. And... with what happened to Sam... And my parents. I lose people. I'm so scared." She felt the sting of tears behind her eyes and reached up to pinch the bridge of her nose. "Oh, God listen to me. This is *your* special time, and I'm ruining it. I'm so sorry. I'm just emotional and tired. Please ignore me."

Josie squeezed her hand. "Hey, we're here for *you* too. If you're worried, you can talk to us. But... maybe you need to talk to Greg. Especially if you know he's worrying about you."

"Yes... yes, I know I do. And I *will* when I get home," she assured her friends. "Look, I'm going to go back to your house. I need to be up early. I'm going to open the shop tomorrow for a while."

"That'll be good for you, I think. Things have been going so well. I'm so sorry for not being there."

Mallory rolled her eyes. "Oh, yeah, Jose. 'Cause you've been so lazy, lying here in hospital giving birth and all that. May just have to fire you." She winked at her friend.

Josie pulled her tongue out. "Sarcastic sod. Now get lost so I can snog my husband in peace."

Mallory smiled. "Don't worry, I'm off. Give that gorgeous son of yours a kiss for me tomorrow, and I'll see you tomorrow night."

CHAPTER 7

Greg rocked back and forth in the pine chair with his baby daughter, Sylvie, in his arms. The restless infant had awoken with an ear-piercing cry at two in the morning. He had finally managed to rock her back to calmness by singing the Bing Crosby classic "White Christmas" in as gentle a voice as his would allow, so as not to wake Mairi.

Yawning, he stood and walked quietly back to the girls' room and placed Sylvie back in her cot. Mairi stirred and snuffled in her sleep—the poor little love was missing her mummy, and he'd had several temper tantrums to deal with in the past couple of days. She was normally such a happy toddler, but with Mallory away, Mairi was certainly finding her voice.

He kissed his finger and touched Sylvie's head

before turning and tiptoeing out of the room to return to his own. Glancing at the clock, he realised it was only three thirty, and he let out a long sigh. Although he was dog tired, he had the feeling that sleep would elude him for the rest of the night.

Other than a couple of texts, he'd heard nothing from Mallory. This only served to exacerbate his overactive imagination. Was she getting tired of him? Was he overreacting? Why hadn't she called? All he wanted to do was to hear her voice; feel a sense of belonging with her once again. But instead here he was in the early hours of the morning, missing her like crazy.

He thought back to their romantic weekend away in the early autumn. Sylvie was three months old at the time, but a pregnant Josie had insisted that she and Brad come to stay and get some practise in before becoming parents for the first time. Greg had jumped at the chance to take his beautiful wife away for a few days to the Scottish Borders. They had stayed in a luxurious hotel on the outskirts of the pretty market town of Kelso.

"I had no idea that this place was so lovely," Mallory said, *looking out the window over the hills and tumbling fields behind the hotel.*

"Aye, that's Scotland for you. A surprise around

every corner." He nuzzled her neck and breathed in her scent. She smelled of roses. Appropriate for his English rose.

"I do love it here," she said dreamily.

"Hmmm... and I do love you."

She turned in his arms and smiled up at him, her bright blue eyes sparkling. "Even though I'm carrying baby weight?"

He pulled his brows in. "Why do you always ask things like that? You've given life to two little girls. Your body is the most amazing thing, Mally. You are amazing. I'm completely in awe of you. And I love every inch of your body. And before you ask, yes, I even love your stretch marks. Do you get it yet? I. Love. You. And I mean forever."

Her eyes glistened with tears, and he sighed heavily. "Oh, great. And now I've made you cry. Can I ever say the right fucking thing?"

She shook her head. "You always say the right thing. I'm sorry, I'm still a bit hormonal, I think."

He bent his head so that his eyes met hers directly. He gazed deep into her blue orbs. "Mally, you are the sexiest, kindest, most beautiful woman I've ever met. And the fact that you've given me two gorgeous daughters just makes me love you more. I've always loved you. I wish you believed me."

She huffed out a breath, making her hair flip upwards. "I do believe you. I really do. Like I said, I'm just hormonal, that's all. And being away from Sylvie is hard. I can't seem to relax."

He bent to kiss her neck, eliciting a moan. Running his hands down her back, he slid his palms over the curve of her bottom and squeezed. She gripped his shoulders and rolled her head back. Sliding his hands up again, he pulled her long-sleeved T-shirt upwards and removed it from her body, discarding it on the floor.

She immediately froze.

Dropping to his knees before her, he unbuttoned her jeans, opening them up to expose her belly. He gazed up into her uneasy eyes as he smoothed his hands up over her hips and gripped her waist. Her fists were clenched at her sides now, and he could see that she was panicked. Dropping his gaze back to her body, he began to trail kisses all over her abdomen, licking and kissing every inch, every stretch mark, and every magnificent imperfection that she had pointed out to him in the previous three months. Sliding his hands into her jeans, he pulled them down along with her panties and nuzzled her mound until her legs trembled...

Thinking about that time filled him with sadness.

The way they had made love that night had been intense and emotional. Things had changed for the better after that, and her confidence had rocketed once again. He couldn't keep his hands off her and she relished his attention. He had made every effort to let her know how desirable she was to him any time the opportunity arose, and even as she gradually lost most of her so-called baby weight, he still lavished attention on the silvery stretch marks left behind. Nothing would stop him from wanting her.

Nothing.

He just wished that he could honestly say he believed Mallory's feelings for him were reciprocal. Over the past month she had become distant. She was staring off into space frequently and spending a lot of time standing on the bridge looking out over the Atlantic. He had tried to talk to her, but she shrugged his worry off and wouldn't open up to him. He wished he could get inside her head. Losing her would break him. But he would never want her to stay with him out of some misplaced loyalty if she were unhappy.

This train of thought terrified him.

Sitting up, he grabbed his phone and hit #1 for her number. His finger hovered over the dial button, and he clenched his jaw. Calling her at this hour would scare her to death. She'd immediately jump to the conclusion that something was wrong, and then when she realised it wasn't and he was just missing her, she'd probably be pissed off.

"Aww, fuck," he growled and put the phone back down on the nightstand. He slammed his body back into the mattress and covered his eyes with both arms, trying his best to relax.

"Daddy! Daddy!" Mairi's sweet little voice woke Greg from his brief sleep. His last glance at the clock had been at five thirty, and it was now only seven o'clock.

"I'm coming, sweetheart." He rubbed his hands over his sore eyes and made his way into the girls' bedroom. Mairi was sitting on her cot-bed, her dark curls wildly sticking out at all angles. A wide smile pulled at the corners of his mouth. *My gorgeous wee girl.* Glancing over to the cot, he could see Sylvie moving too.

No rest for the wicked, eh?

After washing, changing nappies, and dressing his girls, he took them to the kitchen and fed them. As he was finishing up the phone rang.

"Hello?"

"Hey, sweetie, it's me." Mallory's voice was music to his ears and his heart leapt.

"Hey, gorgeous. Are you okay? How's Josie?"

"I'm fine. Josie's awake too. We were at the hospital in the early hours of this morning. I'm exhausted, but I'm going to open up the shop for a few hours today. I think it'll do me good to be back there." *Oh. She wants to be back there. What do I say to that?* "Greg... are you still there?"

Snapped from his worry, he answered, "Aye sorry, sorry. I'm here. Y-yes. That'll be nice, eh?"

"I think so."

"Right well, I've got some work to do today, so Chrissy is coming over at ten to watch the girls."

"Oh, right. What are you off to do?"

"Ron's got a leaky sink. I think a seal has gone, so I've said I'll sort it for him."

"Say hi from me to everyone."

"Aye... I will. Mallory? The girls miss their Mummy."

"Oh, Greg, don't or I'll cry."

"Sorry... Mally?"

"Yes, honey?"

"I... *I* miss you like mad too." A heavy silence fell over the line, and his heart sank. "Mally?"

"I miss you too." She sounded so far away.

CHAPTER 8

After hanging up the call to her husband, Mallory wiped the escaped tears from her eyes. She had awoken to a terrible homesick feeling after a measly three hours' sleep; broken up, of course, by the visit to hospital to see her best friend. After showering and gulping down a cup of coffee, she made her way to the station. Thankfully she didn't have to wait long in the freezing temperatures to catch a train into the centre of Leeds where her gift boutique, Le Petit Cadeau, was situated.

Being back in the city again was strange. It wasn't a place she visited often despite having grown up in the area. Walking from the station to the Victoria Quarter brought myriad memories flooding back. Once again the city centre was a sparkling winter wonderland decked in glitter and bright, festive colours. The fairy lights strewn across the precinct twinkled in the dim morning light as she walked amongst other traders on their way to work.

She wondered absentmindedly why people restricted "good will toward men" to once a year. The atmosphere around the festive season was filled with hope, happiness, and love. How wonderful life would be if this were the case for the other eleven months of the year. December was the month that she met her first real love, Sam and so it was always an emotional contradiction to Mallory.

Arriving at her shop, she rifled through her large handbag to find the keys. Once inside she clicked on the heaters and filled the little kettle at the back. She glanced around the boutique with a sad smile. The business had been set up using the money left to her by her Aunt Sylvia. It had been a dream come true to own her own business, and she had loved meeting new customers as they discovered her handmade artefacts. Being here now *almost* made her miss running the place full-time. But only *almost*. Her life was in Scotland now with her caring, thoughtful—and gorgeous—husband and her two beautiful babies.

Josie had brought in a Christmas CD, and with a smile Mallory hit play. The sound of Chris Rea singing "Driving Home for Christmas" floated around the room, bringing its festive memories of Christmases past. At nine o'clock she turned around her door sign to show that the shop was open, and within five minutes the place was filled with shoppers perusing for last minute gifts.

The cash register was opened and closed just as much as the door, and at lunchtime she was already exhausted. She turned the sign around, grabbed her bag, and dropped the latch behind her as she stepped out into the bustling crowd of frantic, bag-laden shoppers. Turning right, she made her way up the precinct, glancing down to the paving at the spot where she had caught her heel all those years ago and fallen into the arms of her Canadian hunk. If she closed her eyes, she could still smell his cologne...

"Whoaaaa there!" The startled man grabbed for Mallory in a bid to stop her inevitable collision with the pavement. "We haven't been formally introduced, and yet here you are throwing yourself at me." He laughed. His accent was noticeably of the North American variety.

Rather dazed, heart pounding and feeling more than a little bit embarrassed, Mallory slowly lifted her gaze to look at the knight in shining armour, whose strong, muscular arms had come to her rescue. She

LISA HOBMAN

was met with vivid green, laughing eyes and a very, very handsome countenance.

Opening her eyes, she realised she had frozen in place on that fateful spot. People fixed her with confused looks as they sidestepped around her. Shaking her head and pulling her scarf closer around her neck, she continued up to her favourite coffee shop.

As she stood outside the coffee shop to wait while a young couple wheeled out a pushchair, her eyes were drawn to the very table where she and Sam had sat together on the day they met. There was a man sitting there reading a newspaper at an otherwise empty table. As if he felt her eyes on him, he glanced up—and her breath caught. A shiver travelled down her spine and she swallowed hard.

His resemblance to Sam was *uncanny.*

His hair was longer and shaggier and he had a goatee, but he seemed so familiar somehow. His brow creased and he cocked his head to one side in a questioning manner, which caused Mallory to realise that she was staring at the poor guy.

Gulping, she dropped her gaze as heat rose in her cheeks. *Don't be so bloody ridiculous, Mallory, Sam's dead.* She walked through the door and approached the counter but had to pass the man on the way there. A familiar scent infiltrated her nostrils, and her heart leapt as she snapped her eyes to him once again. He was watching her closely with a smile on his face. But rather than the emerald-green eyes of Sam, she was met with the amber eyes of a total stranger. *Great, my mind's playing bloody tricks on me now. Must be tiredness. And face it, lots of men wear that cologne. Now get a bloody grip.* She smiled awkwardly at him and turned to place her order.

Five minutes later, with a takeaway coffee cup and brown paper bag in hand, she turned around to leave. The man who looked like Sam had gone. Feeling relieved that she would be saved from further embarrassment, she made her way outside and walked back toward her shop. She caught sight of the man again, in the distance, walking down the precinct. As she was about to turn into the Victoria Quarter mall, he glanced over his shoulder and made eye contact with her. A chill washed over her and she shivered, turned away, and quickened her pace.

Once inside the shop she made her way into the small restroom at the back. She peered at her reflection in the mirror and was rather disconcerted at the pale face glaring back at her.

"Oh, good grief, please don't let me be coming down with something. Not now. Please," she appealed to the insipid version of herself through the glass. After splashing ice-cold water on her face, she patted it dry with a paper towel.

The doorbell jangled as someone walked in. Rolling her eyes, she muttered, "Oh shit, I forgot to drop the bloody latch." She smoothed down her hair, plastered on a smile, and walked back through to the shop front.

It was *him.*

Okay, this is just unfair now.

"Um... hello, can I help you with anything?" she asked nervously.

He turned to face her and smiled. "Oh, hello. I was just looking, thanks. You have some very lovely and unique things." He had a strange accent that she just couldn't place.

"Thank you." She walked over and sat behind the cash register. "Are you looking for anything in particular?"

He had the most striking eyes. "Not really. Just browsing. You make these?" he asked, pointing at a row of hand-painted signs. The one at the front read, "The past is past. Each day is a new beginning."

"Um... yes. Well, mostly. I buy in from local craftspeople too."

"Well, I must say, you're very talented."

She felt heat bloom from her chest to her cheeks. "Thank you."

A ringing sound emanated from within his coat. "Oooh, sorry, I'd better go and answer that. Merry Christmas." And with no further comment, he left the shop. A feeling of disappointment settled in her stomach as she watched his retreating form.

She half expected the stranger to come back at some point; but every time the door jangled, she glanced up only to be disappointed yet again. She was unsure why his presence was so disconcerting. Perhaps it was just the similarities between him and Sam—and the fact that the last few days had been a whirlwind of comings and goings.

At the end of the day she emptied the cash register of the day's takings and made her way back to the train station. She couldn't help noticing every man in a long black coat that passed her by. But *he* was nowhere to be seen.

Arriving back at Josie and Brad's house, she was greeted with a bear hug that lifted her from the floor and almost extracted her last breath.

"Good grief, Brad. Are you trying to kill me?" she asked as he placed her back on her feet.

"Whoops, soz, Mal. I'm just excited! Josie met our little lad today, and they've said she can come home the day before Christmas Eve. The little one will have to stay in, but we'll visit him on Christmas Day. No doubt armed with loads of prezzies."

It would mean she stayed a day longer in Yorkshire to see Josie settled at home, but Mallory clapped her hands with glee. "Oh, that's wonderful. Have you settled on a name yet?"

His face crumpled. "Let's just say we're in discussions."

She couldn't help smirking. *Typical Josie and Brad.* "Ah. Do I sense a difference of opinion?"

"You could say that. I like Eddie and she likes Zack. So who knows what we'll end up calling him?"

Mallory smiled and shook her head. "You two are an enigma."

He frowned. "What do you mean by that?"

She shrugged. "Well, you hardly ever agree on *anything*, yet you just... *work* somehow."

He pursed his lips for a moment and nodded. "Yeah... I suppose things just have a way of coming right with us."

"So, what's the plan of action for tonight? Am I okay to visit her?"

"I think you'd be in serious trouble if you didn't."

"Great. I'll go shower and grab a sandwich. Are you going too?"

He laughed. "Can't keep me away. I'll drive us."

"Fab. Won't be long." She made her way upstairs to shower and change. Once she reached her room, she picked up her phone and was on the verge of calling Greg with the good news about Josie coming home. As her finger hovered over the dial button, she played a potential conversation over in her mind and decided that she wasn't really ready to discuss the rest of the events of her day. And he would no doubt ask. How could she inform her husband that she'd had a bizarre encounter with someone who looked like Sam?

She couldn't.

She threw her phone back on the bed and walked away.

CHAPTER 9

When Mallory and Brad arrived, the hospital was a hive of activity. She found herself feeling rather sorry for those people who wouldn't be making it home for Christmas, and then her thoughts sprang directly to her husband and two daughters. She missed them terribly, but talking to them would only make the agony of being away from them worse. Shaking off the threatening melancholy, she followed Brad up to the ward where baby Farnham lay in his incubator.

Josie was sitting beside the crib with her hand through an opening, stroking the cheek of her newborn son. A wide smile spread across her face when they walked in. Mallory rushed over and grappled Josie into a hug, taking care not to squash the battered and bruised new mum.

"You look so much better," she informed Josie.

"I feel amazing. And it's all thanks to this little fella. Isn't he gorgeous?"

"Oh, Jose, he's beautiful just like his mum."

"Hey, what about me?" Brad asked sulkily from the other side of the incubator.

The two girls laughed and Josie rolled her eyes. "You've got stiff competition for my affections now, Bradley," Josie informed him with a sly wink to Mallory.

"Yeah, you say that now, but wait 'til you're changing nappies at three in the morning. I'll be the best thing since sliced bread then, when you're begging *me* to do it."

"So, how is he doing?" Mallory whispered as she peered down at the sleeping infant who was attached to monitors and equipment to help him breath. Her breath caught and she chewed on the inside of her cheek to fight the threatening tears.

Josie sniffed. "He's getting stronger. He'll need to stay in for a while, but they've said he's a fighter." Her eyes welled with tears as she spoke, and Mallory's throat tightened too.

"He's strong like his parents," Mallory told them with strong affirmation. She glanced over at Brad, whose gaze was flitting between his son and his wife. He looked so helpless.

"The Reason" by Hoobastank began to float through the air from Mallory's bag. "Oh, heck, sorry, it's Greg calling. I'd better go answer it." She gave an apologetic look to the loved-up couple, but they were oblivious to everything else around them as they stared in wonder at their baby boy. She slunk out of the door and walked down to the TV room.

Putting her phone to her ear, she tried to sound smiley. "Hi, sweetie. Is everything okay?"

"Hi, gorgeous. Yes, yes everything's fine. Mairi just wanted to talk to you."

"Oh, bless her. Pop her on."

There was a muffled, shuffling sound and then snuffling could be heard down the line. "Mummy... come home," came the whiny voice of the two-year-old.

Mallory's heart ached at hearing the little girl's pained voice. "I will soon, darling. Not long now."

"Santa coming soon."

"I know, sweetheart. I'll be back before then. I promise."

"Bye-bye, Mummy. Love you." The little girl was on the verge of tears again.

"And I love you, baby girl. So much."

The shuffling sound came again and then Greg spoke. "She's been inconsolable today. Poor wee girl. I can't seem to get her to understand that you'll be back very soon."

"Well, I'll be home... erm...the day before Christmas Eve hopefully. It'll be late though, so maybe I'll get a cab home."

"That'll cost a fortune, Mally. I'm happy to come and get you."

"No, you stay home with the girls. It's fine."

He let out an audible, frustrated sigh. "You're a bloody stubborn woman, do you know that?"

Smiling, she replied, "Yes, I *know* that. But you love me regardless."

There was a silent pause before he spoke in a low, resigned voice. "Aye... I do... with all my heart."

She scrunched her brow even though he couldn't see her. "You don't sound so happy about that. Is everything okay?"

He huffed. "I could ask you the same question."

"Everything's okay, Greg. Like I keep saying, I'm just tired and emotional. Look... They've said that Josie can come home the day before Christmas Eve... so..."

"So you're staying an extra day."

"Just to make sure she's settled and has everything she needs. And in case Brad needs anything. It's just a day."

"Another day that I don't get to hold you. Another day we don't get to talk, Mally."

Guilt washed over her, but realising that this conversation could end up taking a long while, and that he may begin to probe her about the reasons behind her emotional distance—things she wasn't ready to admit to him—she decided to rush off. "Look, we'll talk when I get home, okay? Now's not the time. I'd better go. Give the girls a cuddle from me."

"Aye... aye, okay. Bye, then."

Mallory sensed the disappointment in his voice and so she tried to lighten the mood. "Bye, chicken pie." She ended the call and immediately realised she hadn't told him she loved him. She was about to call him back when Brad came bursting in through the door.

"Hey, Mal. I've been looking for you. We've done it! We've picked a name!"

"Oh, fab. I'm just coming." She glanced at her phone, suddenly overcome with guilt and contemplating squeezing in a quick text, but Brad was bouncing on the balls of his feet like an excited schoolboy with a new toy. She decided the message could wait a few minutes, and she followed him back to Josie's bedside.

Once inside the room again, Mallory grinned at her friends. "So, you've finally agreed on a name?"

"We have. Good, eh?" Josie answered enthusiastically.

Mallory placed her hands on her hips in faked frustration. "So come on then, the pair of you. Spill it. What do I call my nephew?"

"Well, Aunty Mallory, we would like for you to meet"—Josie briefly glanced up at her beaming husband before looking back to Mallory—"Edward Reid Farnham."

Gazing at the little bundle where he lay looking so small and fragile, Mallory felt tears needle at her eyes.

"It's perfect."

Brad looked down at his wife and child with such love and pride. They made a lovely little family. Mallory bent to place her hand on the transparent covering of the incubator as the sight of the wee baby tugged at her heartstrings and she closed her eyes, suddenly transported back in time to Sylvie's birth.

Exhaustion was evident in Greg's features as he gazed down at his new daughter in her arms. His expression was one of pure adoration, and her heart filled with joy. Such a tough exterior but with a heart full of raw emotion. She reached up and touched his cheek, drawing his attention back to her.

She smiled at her husband. "I know she was a huge surprise, but... my goodness, don't you just love her?"

Tears welled in his chocolate-brown eyes, and his lip trembled. "Aye... I do... with all my heart." His voice broke as he leaned to kiss her tenderly.

When she opened her eyes once more on the present, she spoke with a quivering lip, "Hello baby Edward. Welcome to the world."

CHAPTER 10

The following day Brad was up and off before Mallory was out of bed. She showered, dressed, and made her way down to the kitchen, where she found a note scribbled from Brad.

Morning, Aunty Mal!
I've popped over to the hospital to see my little family. It feels weird saying that let alone writing it! Anyway, I wasn't sure if you were going into the shop again today, but if you are, drop me a text and I'll grab us a takeaway on the way home. Unless you're coming to the hospital later yourself—in which case we can pick up something together.
Sees ya later!
Daddy Brad (couldn't resist that)
XXX

Mallory smiled as she read the note. Brad clearly was the happiest man on earth, and she couldn't blame him for that. She made herself a coffee and drank it leaning against the countertop in her familiar kitchen surroundings. Somehow Brad and Josie's house always felt like home. But at Christmas it made her homesick. Seeing the perfectly decorated tree with its colour coordinated baubles and trinkets made her miss her haphazardly strewn one back in Scotland. Josie was pernickety when it came to her home, and her Christmas tree had always been the same. Where Mallory favoured more traditional ornaments, Josie's tree matched whatever decor she had in place and it seemed to change annually.

Once she had finished her drink, she grabbed her bag and set out for the train that would take her to Leeds city centre. The journey wasn't a long one, and it brought back happy memories of when she'd first set up the shop. It also reminded her of the time she'd gotten stuck on a broken-down train a few years earlier when she was on her way home from Yorkshire to tell Greg that she loved him too—in spite of trying to fight her feelings. The realisation had struck, and she was wrong to try and deny it. Her soul and Greg's had become intertwined back then and she had felt so secure in his embrace. Her heart fluttered at the memory, and she placed her hand there, where Greg had helped her to heal. So many things had changed since then.

After she alit from the train in the early morning half-light, the bitter chill of winter blew down the platform and stung at her cheeks, and she pulled her scarf tight around her neck. Thankfully the walk to the shop wouldn't take long, and she would be putting the heater on as soon as she walked through the door. The city was just waking and getting prepared for the barrage of Christmas shoppers that would be descending as soon as the clock struck nine. As she clip-clopped up the precinct in her unsuitable Mary Janes, the lights in each window became illuminated and the Christmas displays sprang to life, oozing festive cheer even though each one of the shop assistants had probably had her fill by the end of November. Yes, Christmas seemed to be getting earlier.

Once the door of the little gift shop was closed behind her, Mallory flicked on the heat and hit play on the mini hi-fi in the corner. Bing Crosby's voice floated around the room, singing "I'll Be Home for Christmas".

"I will be too, Bing," she told the stereo system as she turned on the lights on the little Christmas tree.

After checking the stock and refilling some of the shelves, she turned the door sign to show Open and took her seat beside the cash register. The Victoria Quarter was already beginning to fill up, and a buzz of excitement thrummed through her veins.

The morning was a busy one with plenty of customers coming in to browse and buy. By the end of the day, Mallory's feet were sore and her head was pounding. She was ready for home... well, Brad and Josie's home anyway. She was just about to close up when a red-haired woman of around twenty-seven came bustling through the door.

"Oh, I'm sorry, are you closing?" she asked with a disappointed expression.

Mallory smiled. "No, you're fine, come on in."

The woman heaved a sigh of relief and stepped further into the shop.

Mallory watched her glance around for a few moments. "Are you looking for anything in particular?"

"Oh... yes, yes, my friend told me I'd get something really special from here... more personal-like for my husband's gift."

Mallory was once again reminded that her little shop touched the hearts of people and that she provided special, unique things that her customers wanted to share with their loved ones. The thought warmed her heart. "Ah, well, that's lovely. What kind of gift did you have in mind?"

The woman smiled dreamily and blushed. "Something that will let him know that no matter how far away he is, he's always in my heart. And that I love him more than anything."

The look of love that took over the woman's features made those pangs of homesickness surface again, and she wondered what Greg and the girls were doing.

After browsing around the shop, the woman picked up a sign that simply said "You're my Prince Charming and we are my happily ever after."

Mallory smiled as she took the gift from the woman's hands to ring it through the cash register. It was one of her own creations. "Is your husband away a lot?" The question slipped out before Mallory considered that she could be prying.

The customer nodded, and her eyes grew watery. "He is. He's in the army and at the moment he's overseas. I don't see him very often right now."

Mallory had the urge to hug the poor woman. She found it difficult being apart from Greg for a few days, and was terrified of losing him, irrational or not —and here was a young wife who faced that very prospect day in and day out. And she wouldn't be able to get her gift to him, Mallory realised. "You do know you've missed last posting for air mail, don't you?"

Brightening up, the red-haired woman told her, "Oh, yes. But our Christmas will be when he comes home in February."

Humbled by the woman's attitude, Mallory began to gift wrap the handmade sign. "Gosh. That must be hard for you. Being so far away from him."

She fumbled in her bag for her wallet. "It is, but... for us, Christmas isn't just about the date in December. It's about being grateful for every minute we get to spend together. Each moment is precious, you know? Let's face it, you never know when it may be your last. And with him being a soldier in active service, I guess we don't ever take each other for granted."

Mallory swallowed hard as a lump lodged in her throat. "Doesn't... doesn't it scare you? The prospect of losing him, I mean?"

The woman smiled and cocked her head to the side. "Yes. Each and every day. But I can't dwell on that. We live in the here and now whenever he's home. And I look forward to every time I can hold him. I make sure he knows how much I love him every single day by text message. And we talk when we can. You can't let fear stop you from living. Well, that's the way I look at it anyway."

The woman handed her payment to Mallory, who placed the wrapped sign in a gift bag and handed it over. "Well, I hope he likes the gift."

"Oh, I know he will. It's beautiful. Thank you so much."

The woman walked out of the shop and Mallory sat down once again. She pulled her own wallet from her bag and gazed at the photograph of Greg and her babies as tears stung at her eyes. Fear was stopping her from living in the here and now. That one thing was certain.

At the end of her very busy but wonderful day, Mallory arrived home to Brad and Josie's at six and went to her room. She rummaged around in her unpacked bag for a warm sweater to wear for her hospital visit when her hands landed upon something hard. She pulled out the mystery object and her breath caught in her throat. It was wrapped in red tissue paper and tied with gold ribbon. *How the heck did that get in here?* She tore at the paper and held the little handmade sign in her hands. The familiar sting of tears prickled at the backs of her eyes as she gazed down at the words.

"Never forget how much we love you." Greg's scrawly, familiar handwriting and two tiny handprints adorned the sage-green painted plaque.

"Oh, Greg," she gasped as the tears overflowed and her heart ached for her family.

CHAPTER 11

Greg stared at the little velvet gift box in his hand. It was a little overdue as gifts go. Eternity rings were supposed to be presented on the birth of the first child, but money had been a little tight and he had wanted to make sure he got the one he wanted. Christine had taken the girls for a walk so he could drive into Oban without the worry of them being with him on the icy roads. He flipped open the lid once again and stared at the white gold band set with seven sparkling princess-cut diamonds. It was a stunning ring and he just knew Mallory would love it. Well, he *thought* she would.

Snapping the box closed, he shoved it in his inside pocket and turned the key in the ignition of the Landy. Before setting off, he flicked through his iPod and found a track list he had made that was filled with songs that reminded him of Mallory. He stared at the illuminated screen as "In the Sun" by Joseph Arthur began to play.

God, he missed her so much. And not just because she was away in Yorkshire. Her emotional distance had been hard to bear and he was desperate to talk things through; but every time he had tried, she had changed the subject. It had got to the point where he was questioning his own sanity. Was he imagining it? No... no, she hadn't seemed herself since Sylvie was born. He had heard of postnatal depression and had been researching it on the Internet, but he knew that diagnosing someone via a website was dangerous and a little silly. He had resolved to sit down with her and get to the bottom of things when she returned. He just hoped she wanted to talk. He couldn't bear losing her.

It would break him.

After a steady drive home, Greg pulled up outside the cottage and cut the engine. He opened the door and climbed out, patting his chest where the ring sat safely inside his jacket pocket. He paused for a moment and took in the view of the bridge from the snow-covered front path. That iconic structure had played such a major role in his life, and he couldn't wait until Mallory crossed it to return to him once again.

A sense of melancholy washed over him as he entered the empty cottage. The fresh scent of pine wafted through from the living room as he closed the front door. He walked through and flicked on the tree lights, hoping their warm golden glow would improve his mood. He'd wrapped all the girls' gifts and hidden them away, meaning that the bottom of the tree was bare. Mairi was too young to really understand about Santa, but he desperately wanted her to feel the magic, and so the presents would be there on Christmas morning. He just hoped that Mallory would make it in time.

He glanced at the clock. Four thirty on the day before Christmas Eve. The fact that Mallory had stayed an extra day in Yorkshire niggled at him. He understood her reasons but couldn't help feeling a little disappointed that her return was being delayed.

After removing his coat and scarf and tossing them onto the couch, he grabbed the little velvet box from the inside pocket and slumped onto the sofa. He opened the box for what felt like the fiftieth time since he'd collected it from the jeweller in Oban and smiled as the stones glinted in the light of the Christmas tree. He wanted to see her eyes light up like they had on the day he had proposed to her on the bridge. All he craved was her happiness; and the fact that she had seemed so lost lately made his heart ache.

He thought back to their honeymoon in Canada when everything had been so perfect. They had stayed in a gorgeous limestone hotel in Kingston's Old Town. Their room had been on the second floor of the beautiful King Street East building, and the sumptuous gold tapestry furnishings, high-quality decoration, and large, ornately carved marble fireplace had oozed luxury. Greg had been relieved that Mallory had suggested the hotel rather than staying at the Buchanans' family home. He adored Renee, but sleeping with Mallory in Sam's old bed would've felt wrong.

The large Jacuzzi bath had been a favourite spot to relax when they weren't sightseeing or shopping, and Greg called to mind one particular occasion that would stick in his mind for all eternity...

He sat, champagne flute in hand, waiting for his new bride. The water was warm and he could feel his muscles relaxing. It was early evening and they had been walking around Kingston all day with Ryan and Cara whilst Renee looked after her grandson. He closed his eyes and let his head rest back onto the bath as the bubbles tickled up his spine.

Eventually he was enveloped by the scent of roses, and heat rushed through his veins. The warmth of her body caressed his naked skin as she entered the water and slid her hand down his chest. He sighed and opened his eyes to gaze up at her. She hovered over him, the water covering her hips, but he was able to feast his eyes on her luscious breasts, and feast he did. Reaching out, he traced the curve of her waist with his fingertips, continuing on to caress her left breast, eliciting a moan that caused his blood to rush south.

"God, you're so, so beautiful, Mallory," he whispered as he met her gaze. A sweet smile turned up her lips and she leaned in toward him and placed her hands on his shoulders. Without a word she moved to straddle his hips and sank her body down, taking him in. He groaned as his eyes fluttered closed for a brief moment. This was a first. They'd made love in the shower but never in a bubbling Jacuzzi. Not that he would ever deny her; she evidently wanted him here and now, and there was no doubt in his mind about his own desires.

He had never loved anyone the way he loved her. He placed his champagne glass down on the side of the bath and gripped her hips as she moved her body over him and pulled her full bottom lip between her teeth. Her hooded eyes closed as she smoothed her hands up and down his chest. Opening them again, she smiled. His heart melted.

His gravelly voice left his body as a low growl. He couldn't believe she was his, and the need to make her understand how lucky he was overcame him. "I love every inch of you, I hope you know that. Your curves, your breasts, your beautiful blue eyes, so clear and expressive. You make me a better man. Loving you has changed me so much." He was aware that he was rambling, but the all-consuming passion and love he had for her bubbling up inside of him, and the intensity of the sensation of her body encompassing him, had his emotions overflowing unabashedly. "I want to love you like this every day. I'll never get enough of you."

She dug her nails into his flesh. "And I'll never get enough of you... the way you make me feel, Greg. This... us together..." Her voice was a lust-filled, breathy whisper.

Hearing her words made his heart soar. He'd wanted this feeling to belong to him since the first time he saw her, and now that she was his, he would make sure never to let her down. Never hurt her.

Never fail her. He owed her so much. She'd taught him how to love completely and irrevocably.

He belonged to her.

She began to tighten around him and he locked his gaze on hers and watched as her orgasm took hold. He felt the sting in his eyes and the love in his heart as he ascended to follow her. Because that's what he would always do. He would follow her anywhere. She was his home now—

A knock on the front door ripped him prematurely from his fantasy, and he wiped at the moisture around his eyes and went to let Christine and his daughters in.

CHAPTER 12

The day of Josie's homecoming had finally arrived, and Mallory had stayed at the house to clean up whilst Brad went to pick up his wife. It had been a frustrating morning to say the least. Brad had been pacing the floor, chewing his nails, checking his phone, pacing some more. Eventually Mallory had set him on changing the bed to keep him occupied before sending him off early to the hospital.

She opened the oven, and the delicious aroma of spiced apple pies wafted from inside. With hands clothed in silicone gloves, she lifted the tray of freshly baked pies out and placed them on a cooling tray. *Hmmm, cinnamon and cloves, the smell of Christmas.* The house was spotless, and a playlist of Christmas music had been on a loop all morning. It was the turn of Slade, singing "Merry Christmas Everybody", and Mallory was dancing around the room feeling particularly festive. It was December 23, and Mallory was looking forward to returning home to her family the following day. She'd had little contact with Greg, unsure what to say to him about her frame of mind of late, and had resolved to set things right as soon as she arrived back in Scotland.

Baby Edward was gaining strength each and every day, and Brad had spent every possible moment with his wife and baby son. Mallory had been plagued by homesickness, but the nightmares about losing Greg had become less frequent. She walked back through to the living room and picked up the photos from the mantel one by one, smiling as she recalled the happy times they had spent as a group of friends. It had become a tradition to have a photo take in front of the Christmas tree each year, and Mallory was saddened that this year it wouldn't be the full gang in the shot.

She placed the last photo frame down and flopped onto the sofa, taking in the clean and fresh surroundings and happy that she had been able to help. As she stared at the twinkling lights of the tree, she was transported back in time to her second Christmas with Sam. They had met the year before, and he had spent their first Christmas in Canada, but their second was a special one indeed. They were living together in railway cottage...

"*The turkey won't be long, it's just resting.*" *Mallory blew the hair out of her eyes as a bead of sweat trailed down her forehead and dripped off the end of her nose.*

"*Honey, why won't you let me help you?*" *Sam asked as he leaned against the doorframe, trying to stifle a grin.*

"*Because... I want this to be a special meal for you. I want to cook for you.*"

She flung a dish towel over her shoulder and grabbed a fork. Digging it into the Brussels sprouts, she decided they were done.

Sam's arms came about her waist and he nuzzled her neck, sending shivers down her spine and eliciting a moan.

"*You made Brussels sprouts.*"

"*I did,*" *she replied with a smile.* "*Ryan told me they're your favourite part of Christmas lunch, and so I wanted to make it extra special.*"

He nibbled at her earlobe. "*Awww, baby, you're so sweet.*"

She sighed and her eyelids fluttered closed. "*Keep that up, and lunch will be ruined.*"

Sam chuckled and moved away. Mallory huffed sulkily despite knowing that if he had continued, they would have ended up making love right there in the kitchen.

The table was set and a red candle was lit in the middle of a small Christmas garland at the centre of the table. The cloth was Stewart tartan and the place mats gold. Mallory put serving dishes full of boiled sprouts, roast parsnips, baked sprouts with roast potatoes, stir-fried sprouts, sage and onion stuffing, and pigs in blankets with an extra addition of sprouts, on the beautifully laid table. Sam walked through from the living room and took his seat opposite Mallory. She carved the succulent white meat and placed it on his plate, a sense of pride washing over her at his wide smile.

Sam poured champagne into two crystal flutes and handed one to Mallory. He raised his glass. "To my beautiful girl and to many more Christmases together."

Mallory clinked his glass with her own and sipped the bubbly liquid as she smiled at him. He returned her smile with a look of sheer adoration. To add to the warm, festive glow, Nat King Cole sang "The Christmas Song", his smooth-as-silk voice drifting through the house.

Mallory placed her glass on the gold coaster beside her. "Go on, dig in before it goes cold."

Sam piled his plate high with food, and Mallory's stomach flip-flopped. Would he like it? Would it actually be edible? Unable to draw her gaze away, she watched as he took a forkful of food and popped it into his mouth. He chewed and his expression changed. Oh God, he hates it.

She bit back her panic. "What... what's wrong, Sam?"

He shook his head and swallowed. What looked like a forced smile appeared on his face. "Nothing, babe. It's delicious."

Mallory stuck out her bottom lip like a spoiled child. "You're lying. It's awful, isn't it?"

He placed his fork down, and his cheeks turned pink as he stared at his plate.

She took a deep breath. "Come on. Admit it."

He brought his face up and met her gaze. "Um... you know how Ry told you I love sprouts?"

She nodded slowly. "Ye-e-e-es?"

"I'm sorry, honey, but he was kidding around. I hate them. The way they look, the smell, the texture, and oh, God, the taste." He shivered. "The rest of it is absolutely delicious, no word of a lie. Cross my heart." He made the cross sign on his chest.

She opened and closed her mouth like a goldfish. "I'll... I'll bloody get him for this. What a shit."

Sam's eyes sparkled as he broke into fits of laughter. "Yup. He got me good. He knew I'd just eat them anyway."

Mallory stood from her seat and walked around the table. She sat on Sam's lap and slipped her arms around his neck. "You'd have done that... for me?"

He reached up and cupped her cheek. "Baby, I would do anything for you."

Her heart melted as she leaned in to kiss him. He was so wonderful...

The front door opened, pulling Mallory from her reverie. A pale-looking Brad walked in and Josie hobbled closely behind him.

"Mally, will you tell him I'll be bloody fine? He's driving me nuts already." Josie sounded distinctly pissed off, and Mallory couldn't help but laugh.

"Mally, can you tell your best friend here that my offering to carry her in is in no way me insinuating that she's a weakling and needs mollycoddling." Brad was evidently just as pissed off as his stubborn wife.

Mallory shook her head. "How about I go put the kettle on, and you tell *each other* your bloody complaints?" She laughed to herself as she walked away.

Seeing the two of them back to their usual banter was a huge relief. Everything had felt so uncertain there for a while, and it was clear that they had been handling each other with kid gloves. If only her own relationship worries could be resolved as easily. Her laughter ceased as she contemplated trying to explain her irrational fears to Greg. To her they weren't irrational at all. But how could she make Greg see that the reason she was so scared was *because* of how much she loved him and not the contrary, as he was clearly assuming?

Mallory's train was booked for eight o'clock the following morning. It was such a long journey, and travelling home on Christmas Eve was not the best idea she had come up with; but because Josie had been released from hospital much earlier than expected, she had stayed an extra day. The new mum had been very tearful about being at home whilst her little boy fought to get stronger in the hospital, and that wouldn't change for several weeks... maybe longer. She kept thanking Mallory for being by her side whilst Brad fretted and fussed around her like a mother hen. Bless him, he was just so protective of his wife after what she'd been through to bring their son into the world, and he couldn't really be blamed for that.

It was a chilly morning, and the sky looked heavy with an imminent snowfall. Mallory made sure to leave her warm, woolly scarf out of her small case.

Josie appeared at the door. "Are you all ready to go, hon?"

Mallory smiled, but the feeling didn't accompany the expression. "I am. Will you be okay? You've been through such a lot. And with Edward still being in the hospital, maybe—"

"Maybe you should stop worrying and get home to that grumpy-arsed husband of yours and those gorgeous girls."

Mallory opened her mouth, feeling rather affronted at Josie's words. "He's not grumpy-arsed, Jose. Take that back."

Josie chuckled. "I knew you'd defend him. You know why that is?"

Mallory folded her arms across her chest. "Why?"

"Because you worship the bloody ground he walks on, and he feels the same about you. So get yourself back up to Scotland and jump his bones."

Mallory felt blood rush to her cheeks. "God, you're so crass."

Laughter erupted from her best friend. "Oh, come off it. You're not a bloody prude. I reckon you need a bloody good shag."

Mallory tried not to laugh but eventually gave in and whacked her friend with a pillow.

"Taxi's here, Mally," Brad called from the living room. Mallory placed her coffee mug in the sink and followed Josie through to where Brad stood.

She shrugged on her coat and grabbed her scarf, wrapping it around her neck. "Give that little boy a kiss from me when you go today." Her voice broke with the emotion of leaving her friends.

Josie flung her arms around her and squeezed her tight. "Go get things sorted at home. Stop worrying and just be happy, okay?"

Mallory nodded wordlessly into Josie's shoulder. "I just hope he'll forgive me."

"Don't be daft. Of course he will. He'll completely understand." Josie pulled away and made direct eye contact with Mallory. "Think about it, Mally. The last five years have been a bloody roller coaster. The death of a lovely man, falling in love with another, giving birth to two babies. It's enough to drive any woman over the edge. Maybe you should speak to your doctor. You may be suffering postnatal depression."

Mallory had never even considered that possibility. "I've nothing to be depressed about. I've so much to be thankful for, and it'd be pathetic if I were depressed."

Josie tucked a strand of hair behind Mallory's ear. "Mally, depression is a real illness. It's not you being pathetic. It's you experiencing a hell of a lot in a short period of time and your hormones being all out of whack. It doesn't mean you're weak. I've researched this during my own pregnancy. I really think you should see someone, hon."

She didn't want Josie to be right, not about this. But perhaps she was. Mallory was a mother, after all, and so she couldn't rule it out entirely. She nodded and pulled Josie into her arms again. "I will, I promise. And you take care. Don't do too much. You've had major bloody surgery and you shouldn't even be walking around."

"Oh, God, don't get like Brad," Josie mumbled into Mallory's shoulder. She laughed lightly.

Mallory pulled away and smiled at her friend. "I love you, you know."

"And I love you too, you daft bat."

After Mallory hugged Brad and then Josie one more time, she left the house and climbed into the waiting cab.

CHAPTER 13

The journey to the station seemed to take forever, and it gave Mallory far too much time to think. Josie's words rattled around her head. Depression was something she had never experienced before, so there was no reason she would recognise the symptoms. *If* she had it. She connected to the train's wireless service and typed the word into the search engine bar.

She scrolled through page upon page of text, and after half an hour of reading, she had resolved to contact her GP on her return home. Depression wasn't something she wanted for herself, yet as she realised that her irrational fears, insomnia, and feelings of helplessness were all explainable, a sense of relief filled her.

Flicking to a weather site, she decided to look

and see if there was any reason for her journey to be delayed—but when she read the report she regretted it instantly. Storms and heavy snow had been forecast for the duration of the journey. *Oh, great.* All she wanted was to be at home with Greg and her girls. But the fear that something terrible could happen to *her* hit like a freight train. *How would Greg cope? And the babies? Oh, good grief.* Hitting the off button, she rubbed her hands over her face. Was this part of depression too? Worrying about things she couldn't control before they actually happened? Was it normal to worry about things like storms and travel? She resolved that this was something that needed investigating further. She couldn't deal with it alone.

That realisation in itself brought its own sense of relief.

The train's catering staff wheeled a trolley down the aisle, and Mallory bought herself a piece of shortbread—to remind herself of home—and a coffee. Munching on the buttery biscuit, she smiled as she stared out the window at the monochrome landscape that spread for miles beyond the train's windows.

Snowflakes fluttered to the white ground with gaining speed, and she was thankful of the warm drink before her. The train was less busy than she expected, and gradually, the further north they travelled, the fewer people remained in the carriage.

Once she had finished her coffee, she thumbed through the magazine she had bought at the station. It was filled with Christmas recipes and homes decked out in festive colours. A warm, fuzzy feel of excitement settled over her as she stared at a particularly heart-warming scene of a family. It could've been a glimpse into the future of her own little family. Two little girls with dark, curly hair sat beside a tree adorned with red, gold, and green. The dad wore an embarrassing Santa jumper, and the mum watched her daughters with a look of adoration. Mallory couldn't wait to see Greg's face on Christmas morning when he opened his gift. She had bought him a framed Flick MacDuff print of a village in the Highlands called Sheildaig. She'd decided that she would take him there for a romantic weekend away once the girls were a little older. The magazine held her interest for a few minutes longer, then she set it down.

The trouble with long train journeys was the boredom. Mallory spent a while reading her book until a headache began to throb at her temples. The lack of decent sleep was taking its toll, and sleeping in a bed alone hadn't helped. She'd missed the feel of Greg's arm possessively draped over her at night.

She managed to force down a packet of crisps and a cheese sandwich when the trolley came around with lunch, and her head eased a little, and so she pulled out her book once again.

The train arrived at another station along the way, and further down the train, a group of drunken revellers boarded and proceeded to sing "When Santa Got Stuck up the Chimney" at the top of their voices. Mallory didn't know whether to laugh or be pissed off. Luckily the group alighted at the next station, and a peaceful calm settled over the train once again.

Several hours had passed, and Mallory had finished her book. She rested her head back onto her seat and closed her eyes. *Perhaps a nap will make the journey go quicker, and then I can be back with Greg and my girls.*

The next time she opened her eyes, the sky had darkened. She figured she must have been dozing for a couple of hours. As she glanced around, she realised that she was the only passenger left in her carriage. Reaching upwards, she stretched as a yawn escaped. She turned to the window to see where the train might be—and gasped.

As she stared wide-eyed through the glass at the depth of snow that blurred the landscape, Mallory's heart thundered as the snowfall came thicker and faster. Suddenly the train ground to a halt, the lights flickered, and she glanced nervously around her. The first-class carriage was all but empty, and the shiver that traversed her spine emphasised the eeriness of being alone.

A guard walked into the carriage and stopped beside her. "I'm so sorry, madam, but we appear to have lost power, and the track up ahead is completely covered in snow." The worried expression on his face made her heart thump harder.

"Oh... I see. Should I get off and go find a hotel or something?"

"Oh, gosh, no. Please don't do that. We're on a two-track bridge. It'd be dangerous for you to disembark up here."

Stuck on a bridge? Huh. What is it with me and bridges? "So... what happens now?"

"Well, I'll bring you a warm drink and... and a blanket. Perhaps it would be a good idea to try and sleep."

Her stomach churned and dread filled her. "But... I can't... I have to get home." Her words tumbled out faster and faster. "It's Christmas Eve and I've promised my daughters and husband I'll be there for Christmas."

"I understand, dear. I really do. I want to get home too. But unfortunately, until we can get an engineer out here, we're... um... rather stuck."

Her lip began to quiver and she turned away from the guard. Searching through her bag, she grabbed her phone. "Right... well, I'd better let them know I may not be there, I suppose." Glancing down at her handset, she realised there was no signal, and to top it off her battery was low. "Oh, great! This is just bloody great." She sighed. It didn't make her feel any better, so she slammed her bag down on the seat beside her, which didn't improve her mood either. She rested her head back, and closed her eyes, pulling in a long breath that she hoped would go some way to calming her down.

"I'll... I'll leave you to it. I'm so sorry," the man said before walking away down the train.

"Is this seat taken?" The voice was vaguely familiar, and she opened her eyes.

Her jaw fell open. "You?" How come the amber-eyed stranger kept on turning up unannounced?

He glanced around and then down at his body. "Yes, I think it's me." He smiled. "So, may I sit? I don't know about you, but being on here alone is creeping me out."

Returning his smile, she gestured to the empty space. "Oh, sure... yes, you can sit."

"Great. Thanks." He slipped into the seat opposite and folded his hands in front of him on the table. "I wonder how long we'll be stuck here."

Mallory huffed. "Oh, God, not long, I hope. My family is waiting at home for me."

He shook his head. "Not good. Not good. Let's hope we're moving again soon then, eh?"

There was a long pause as she turned to look out of the window at the blizzard surrounding the train. "Are you on your way home too?"

"You could say that," he replied with a half-smile.

Okay, so we're going with cryptic answers, then? "I can't quite believe this has happened. The blizzard came out of nowhere."

His amber eyes sparkled with mirth. "Yes, the timing wasn't great. It's typical, isn't it? People in this country spend all their lives hoping for a white Christmas, and when it happens, it's at the most inconvenient time."

She laughed at the irony. "You've got that right."

Sitting back in his seat, he turned to gaze out the

window. "I used to love snow. Where I grew up, we used to get snowed in every year."

"Goodness. How did you cope with that?"

"We used to sled everywhere. Or ski. It wasn't so bad."

She raised her eyebrows. "It actually sounds like fun."

"It was, mostly."

"So... are you heading to Scotland?"

"Not quite. I'm heading north though."

"Is your family waiting for you?"

A smile played upon his full lips. "Some of my family, yes. My... my dad mainly."

"Oh, how lovely."

He nodded. "Yes. Christmas is a time for families, don't you think?"

"Absolutely. That's why I'm so upset that I may not get home to my girls."

"How old are they... your girls?"

"One is two and one is six months." She smiled fondly as she thought about them.

"Oh, wow. Such cute ages. Are they both as beautiful as their mom?" She felt the blush rise in her cheeks and just knew that she was as red as beetroot. He pulled his lips in briefly. "Sorry, that was a little inappropriate, I suppose."

"No, it's fine. And they are very beautiful... but I don't know that they get it from me. Their father is—he's—" Her heart fluttered as Greg popped into her mind, shirtless in all his tattooed glory. Damp from a shower, droplets of water glistening on his smooth skin. She swallowed. "They have their father's eyes," she managed to say.

He smiled and nodded knowingly. "That's sweet."

The two newly not-so-acquainted companions sat in silence for a few minutes until the guard returned. "Here you go, madam." He handed her a blanket and she pulled it around herself. "Would you like a hot chocolate? Or tea... coffee, perhaps?" he asked.

"Hot chocolate would be good, thank you."

"Okay, I won't be long, madam." He turned and dashed off once again.

Mallory scrunched her brow. "How rude." She watched as the man disappeared down the train. "He didn't even offer you anything."

"Oh, don't worry. I had one earlier. I think I was sitting nearer to the buffet car when they came around the first time. Maybe he hadn't realised you were down here by yourself when he came around then. Poor guy looks flustered."

She suddenly felt guilty for thinking so badly of the man. "Yes... maybe so. I feel terrible now. He's missing his family too."

The handsome stranger leaned forward and tilted his head to one side. "Hey, don't beat yourself up. This is a stressful situation to be in. I'm sure he'll be fine. An engineer will come, and we'll be moving again before you know it."

Mallory knotted her fingers. "I hope so. I'll be glad to get home."

"I bet you will."

"Yes... Things have been a little strange lately."

"How come?"

She gave a nervous laugh. "Oh, good grief. You don't want to hear all my woes."

He glanced around the carriage. "I don't seem to have any other pressing engagements right now."

She sniggered. "Fair point."

"And as for me being a stranger... sometimes it's good to get things off your chest to someone you're likely never to meet again."

She pursed her lips for a moment. "Also a good point. But you seem to forget that we've bumped into each other in bizarre circumstances several times over the last week."

He smirked. "Okay, now *you*'re making a fair

point. But... well, let's face it, it doesn't look like we're going anywhere fast, does it? And unless you want to play I spy, I think we may as well talk."

She laughed at the suggestion of I spy. "Oh, yes, can you imagine? I spy with my little eye something beginning with s... snow... snowflake... snowdrift."

His responding chuckle was deep and genuine. "Exactly my point. So... you were saying?"

"Oh... it's such a long story. My... my husband and I met under odd circumstances a few years ago now."

"Hmmm... it seems you like to meet people under odd circumstances."

"Yes, I do seem to make a habit of that."

He smiled again and gestured for her to continue. "Go on... I'm intrigued."

"I met someone... years ago... in Leeds. We fell in love. He was... he was *everything* to me. We were going to move to Scotland to start a new life together, but"—she wasn't sure she really wanted to open up like this to a perfect stranger, but the words rushed out—"on the day we moved, he was snatched from me... A car accident. It was so sudden, such a shock. I don't think I ever fully recovered."

She gazed out at the snow again as the pain of losing Sam stabbed at her heart and she swallowed the rising lump in her throat. "Greg... my husband... was working in the village I moved to. We... we became friends first. He'd lost someone he loved too, and so we shared a common grief, I suppose." She glanced up at her companion, who was listening intently. "Please tell me if I'm boring you senseless."

He shook his head. "Not at all. Please... go on."

She blew out a long sigh and dabbed at her eyes. "He fell for me quickly... Greg, I mean. But... I was racked with guilt at the feelings I'd started to have for him. I'd only just lost Sam. It felt so... *wrong*. Far too soon. It took me almost losing Greg too in a boating accident to realise I actually did love him."

"Fear can do strange things to you," the stranger interjected thoughtfully.

"It can. The trouble is—oh, God, listen to me rambling on."

The guard appeared in the doorway and walked steadily down the carriage with a steaming mug. She decided to stop talking until the man had gone. The last thing she needed was for him to hear her grumbling about her life when he too was stuck on this train, trying to keep everyone happy.

He placed the mug down before her. "There you go, madam. I'll pop back and give you an update as soon as I can."

"Thank you. That's very kind," she replied. He smiled, turned, and walked back down the train once again. "Poor guy. He looks so... dejected," she observed.

The stranger briefly followed her gaze before turning back to her. "He'll be fine. I just know it. So... you were saying?"

She pursed her lips. "Honestly, it's fine. It's weird telling you all this. I don't know you from Adam."

His wide, handsome smile was disarming. "No, but in case you haven't noticed, I'm a very good listener."

He had a good point... again. But the thought crossed her mind that he could be a psychopath for all she knew. As if reading her mind, he leaned forward and said, "Look, I'm just a normal friendly guy stuck on a train. This could turn out to be a long night. You don't have to give me any details that would identify you once we leave this train. Think of me as... oh, I don't know... a sounding board. Impartial. Non-judgemental."

She eyed him warily for a few silent moments. "Okay. No names or locations. No other info."

"Fine by me. Just talk and I'll listen. You were saying that things have been strange lately."

LISA HOBMAN

She sighed again. "Yes... The trouble is... I think I'm... *scared.*" Saying the words out loud helped her to realise her fear was a real, palpable thing. An entity that was hell bent on stopping her from living in the here and now.

The man cocked his head to one side again. "Scared of what?"

The snow outside the window wasn't easing, and the white-out was eerie in its bleakness. "Well, I lost Sam, and I nearly lost Greg once too. Now that we have our beautiful children, I'm absolutely terrified of losing them... *or* him. It's like I've gone into some kind of... I don't know... self-preservation mode."

His brow pulled in. "How do you mean?"

"I think I've started to push him away. I've started to distance myself. He's noticed too. He's been trying to talk to me, but I've been avoiding the issue. It's like I somehow think that, subconsciously, pulling away will make things easier if I *do* lose him." Her throat tightened and her chest began to ache as she expressed her innermost fears out loud.

"But what makes you think you'll lose him?"

"Because I *lose* people. Things are going well, and then people die. My parents, my aunt, my Sam... and almost Greg too."

"But you hit the nail on the head there."

She shook her head in confusion. "I... I don't get what you mean."

"You *almost* lost Greg. But he's still *there*. At home waiting for you. With your children. He hasn't gone *anywhere*."

He was right. "No... you're right. But what if something happens?"

Looking straight into her eyes, he leaned forward again and placed his hand on her arm where it rested on the table between them; his touch was warm and comforting somehow. "Look... take it from someone who knows... life happens. *Shit* happens. Life can be very cruel, and the people you love can be snatched from you without a word of warning. Life can literally throw you off balance when you least expect it. But that's the way life *is*. You *have* to make the most of the people you love. Make sure they know how much you love them at *every* opportunity. Enjoy *every minute* you get with them. Because if they *are* taken from you, it's those memories that help you get through life. The memories of the silly things like... like walks in the woods, or standing together looking at a beautiful view. Keeping each other warm when it's cold out. Laughing at some silly Monty Python sketch. Those little memories are the things that keep people alive in your heart. If you close yourself down through fear, you'll miss out on so much."

The pain in his amber eyes seemed to catch fire. He clearly had lost someone just like she had.

He squeezed her arm gently. "You have to think about all the wonderful times you shared with Sam. If you'd known you were going to lose him, would you have changed any of the moments you shared? Would you have stepped back? Would you *not* have pursued a relationship with him?"

She shook her head emphatically. "Absolutely not. No way. I don't regret a single moment of being with him."

He smiled as if her answer pleased him. "Well then, you have your answer for your current situation. Greg adores you. He must. He waited for you. He took care of you and stood by you when you lost Sam. He shared your grief. You said he's worried that you're becoming distant. Tell him why. Explain how you feel. He'll understand your fears, I can guarantee it. And then once you've talked, you need to move forward with your lives. Don't let *anything* stand in the way of your happiness with him. Don't dwell on what *might* happen or what might have been. Deal with what *does* happen *when* it happens. And if, God forbid, you *do* lose him, you wear bright colours and celebrate the good times you shared."

Her heart pounded as his words sank in. And the way he described what they had done at Sam's memorial was so startlingly similar that memories came flooding back. But he was right. She was holding back and wasting her life worrying about things she couldn't control.

It was time to stop.

It was time to look forward, not dwell on the past.

The love she had shared with Sam had been amazing and deep, but the love she shared with Greg was those things too. She loved him with all of her heart. Sam was her past, but Greg and her daughters were her future.

Sitting up straighter in her seat, she smiled her thanks. Her vision was a little blurry with tears. "Do you know what? I think you're right."

Suddenly the train began to move. Turning to look out of the window, she noticed that the snowfall had almost stopped and stars glimmered in the night sky once again. The heavy clouds that had shielded the moon from sight were now dissipating, and hazy white light cast an ethereal glow over the snow-covered fields and distant hills.

The companions sat in silence for a while as the train trundled along the track. Once off the bridge, they watched as the passing scenery became something befitting a Christmas card. Mallory wished that the train could go faster and get her home to her wonderful husband sooner.

But she would have to be patient.

"So what are your plans for Christmas Day?" she asked.

"Oh... you know. Spend some quality time with Dad. Reminisce a little."

"That sounds nice."

"Yeah..."

"I hope you have a wonderful time with your dad."

He smiled fondly. "I always do."

Silence fell over them again, but every so often, Mallory glanced over at her companion. Sometimes he was watching her with a serene smile and sometimes he was gazing into the distance, the same smile fading and reappearing as if he were lost in thought.

Mallory pulled her phone from her purse. She needed to let Greg know that she would be delayed and he wasn't to worry. Checking the signal, she realised there was none, and so she closed her eyes for a while and thought back to her early days with Greg. The CD of songs he'd made for her... the first night she spent in his arms... the very first time they made love... his romantic proposal on the bridge... the wedding in the small but stunning Kilbrandon Church. Each moment had been perfect because of Greg. He had always put her first. Even when his actions were misguided, he had been doing things out of his love for her.

Fear was such a crippling emotion. It was time to step into the light and leave the fear of loss behind. She would be eternally grateful to her companion for his words of wisdom. Remembering another train journey, she gave a little laugh. The elderly lady who had convinced her to take a chance with Greg all those years ago had been right. *Maybe strangers on trains have some kind of ingrained wisdom*, she thought. *At least I know where to go for advice in future.*

A while later the train pulled into a station in the Scottish Borders. Even that brought to mind a break Mallory had spent there with Greg. He was such a huge part of her life. He *was* her life. The urge to speak to him now was overwhelming, and she even considered dashing off to call whilst the train was at a standstill but knew that, realistically, there would be no time. He'd be so worried, and after what she'd put him through lately, she hated being the cause of more upset for him.

Her companion stood. "Well, this is me."

A wave of sadness washed over her. "Oh... right. Well, have a lovely Christmas. And thank you so much for listening to me ramble on. I really appreciate it. You made a lot of sense."

He smiled sadly and nodded. Putting his hands in his pockets, he turned to walk away but stopped. "Take care, Mallory. Be happy... always."

She smiled as he disembarked from the train and walked off into the darkening winter evening. The train heaved forward again, and as the dimly lit station disappeared into the distance, she thought back to their conversation. She scrunched her brow. He had called her Mallory. *So much for not telling him my name.* She racked her brain, trying to remember at what point she had revealed her identity but couldn't bring it to mind at all. *Definitely losing the plot lately.* She smiled to herself and shook her head.

CHAPTER 14

Eventually at eleven o'clock the train pulled into Oban station. It had been a long journey in more ways than one. Mallory pulled her bag from the overhead locker, placed it on the seat before her, and shrugged into her coat. Collecting the gift-laden bag again, she made her way down the train. The guard who had brought her hot chocolate and a blanket was standing near to the door. She decided that she should thank him and wish him a merry Christmas.

A warm, friendly smile spread across his pale features as he watched her approaching. "We made it eventually, madam," he said as he held his hands out from his sides.

"We did. I wanted to say thank you for the hot chocolate and blanket. I didn't sleep, but the blanket was very much appreciated. It got quite chilly in the carriage."

He chuckled. "I can imagine." He dropped his gaze for a moment, and when he lifted his eyes to meet hers again, they were filled with something that distinctly looked like guilt. "Look, I'm sorry I left you all alone down there. If I'd been a *true* gentleman, I would've sat with you for a while when I brought your drink. Instead I just left you there... all alone in an empty train carriage."

A cold shiver began at the nape of her neck and tingled down her stiffened spine. "But... I wasn't alone... I had—"

"You're being too kind to me. I *did* leave you alone. And I feel very bad about that. You looked so lost and very emotional when I brought the blanket and hot chocolate. It was cruel of me to leave you there like that. The least I could've done was to keep you company. You were the only person on the train who was in that situation. The few people up at the other end seemed to be in couples or groups. But you sat there... cold and by yourself. I'm so, so sorry. A single lady passenger being left like that..." He shook his head. "I should've left the others to fend for themselves. But they were quite a demanding bunch."

Mallory pulled her brows in as confusion swept through her like a cold chill. "When... when you were up at the other end... did you serve a man in a long black coat? Piercing amber eyes. Shaggy, mousy hair and a goatee? Maybe about my age?"

He frowned and shook his head. "Sorry, no. It was all old folks coming home from a Turkey and Tinsel getaway down in Yorkshire. Although why they would want to travel all that way for Christmas dinner beats me, and to be travelling home on Christmas Eve—crazy idea as far as I'm concerned. There's nothing like being home at Christmas, if you ask my opinion."

Gulping as her heart raced, she tried to make sense of her thoughts. "I—I could've sworn I saw a man fitting that description," she said with a wavering voice as realisation began to set in.

"Sorry, dear. I can describe *each* and *every* blue rinse, perm, and set of false teeth I've encountered on this train tonight. And I can safely say that *he* wasn't here. Maybe he caught a different train and will meet you tomorrow?" he offered, not fully understanding the weight of her situation.

She nodded. "Erm... yes... yes, maybe."

He touched her arm as concern masked his features. "Are you okay? You've gone very pale.

You look like you've seen a ghost." He smiled warmly.

She dropped her gaze to the floor for a few moments until she realised he had asked her a question. "Sorry?" Her eyes snapped up to the guard's once again. "Oh, yes... yes, I'm fine. Just... tired, I think."

She wrapped her scarf around her neck and stepped carefully from the train, wishing the man a merry Christmas as she did so. *What the hell just happened?* She walked along the platform toward the exit in a daze.

She pulled out her phone, intending to let Greg know she'd arrived in one piece, but her finger hovered over his number and then dialled Josie. It was late, but the fact that she was a new mother would no doubt mean she was either feeding her son or too excited or terrified to sleep.

As luck would have it, she answered after two rings. "Hey, sweetie! I've been trying to call you. It kept going to voicemail and I was so worried."

"Yes... sorry. It's been quite an eventful journey. I... I lost signal, and the train broke down for a while."

"Are you home now?" Josie asked hopefully.

"N-not yet. Just going to get a cab. Can I ask you a completely ridiculous question?"

Josie laughed. "This is me you're talking to. If you didn't, I'd be worried."

"Okay... here goes... Do you believe in... in ghosts?"

There was a long pause at the other end of the line. "Honestly? I... I'm not sure. I think that there must be something... but... Why do you ask? Is everything okay?"

"I'm not sure. I had a rather bizarre experience on the train."

"With a ghost?"

The change in pitch of her friend's voice made Mallory suddenly feel very foolish. "Oh, good grief. I think I'm so tired that I'm imagining things. It's stupid. I was chatting to a lovely man in the first class carriage, but... when I got off, the guard..."

"Mally? The guard what? Was a ghost? Have you been watching *The Polar Express* with the girls, hon?"

"No... no. Not the guard. Look, forget I said anything. I'd better go."

"Mally, tell me. I know something is off with you. Come on. What is it?"

Mallory sighed deeply. "When I got off the train,

the guard apologised for leaving me alone in the carriage. But... but I *wasn't* alone. He brought me a hot chocolate and a blanket whilst I was chatting to that nice man. Why would he apologise for leaving me alone? And why when I described the man to the guard did he say that no one fitting that description was on the train? Am I... Am I going doolally, Jose?"

A heavy silence fell over the line.

After a few moments Josie spoke. "What... what did the man look like?"

Mallory called to mind the stranger's features. "Shaggy hair, beard. Oddly enough, he reminded me of Sam. But not exactly. Not completely like Sam. If you know what I mean?"

"Did he have amber eyes?" Josie asked quietly.

Mallory widened her eyes. "Yes! How did you know that?"

"He... he was in my dream. The one I had about you and Greg splitting up. He told me to tell you—"

Another shiver travelled down the length of Mallory's spine. "What did he ask you to tell me?" Tears stung at her eyes.

"He just told me to tell you that you were always meant for Greg... and to tell you... to be happy... always."

Mallory suddenly felt very light-headed and

faint. She collapsed against the wall behind her. "The man—the stranger—he said the same words to me as he left the train."

"Oh my God, Mally. I've gone cold. Are you okay? Do you need me to come up?"

Mallory laughed, adoring the fact that her best friend had suggested such a ludicrous thing in her current state. She really was a good friend. "Josie, you've just been through surgery and given birth. Don't be a silly arse. I'll be fine. It's... it's just a coincidence. There has to be some reasonable explanation for all this. We're so close as friends that we're probably in tune with each other's dreams. That's all it'll be. I'm just tired, and you've been through so much. Get some rest. I'll call you tomorrow."

"Okay... are you sure you're alright?" Josie's voice wavered.

Tears spilled over and made cold, wet trails down Mallory's cheeks. "I'm fine. I just want to get home to Greg and the girls."

"I bet you do. Look, Mally, I'm sorry I didn't mention this before. I just thought it was a dream. You know?"

"Yes... yes, that's *all* it was. Don't worry. Love you, and merry Christmas." Mallory hit the end call button and swiped the tears away with the back of her hand. She glanced down at her handset through the fog of her tears and realised the battery had died. *Dammit!* She snuffled and thought back to what had happened over the last few hours. What the hell should she make of all this? She had no idea, but what she did know was that seeing as her phone wasn't an option, getting home to show Greg how much she loved him was paramount.

As she left the station building, she saw a man hailing a passing cab. *Oh, dammit again, if I'd been a few minutes earlier, that could've been mine.* She walked along the road, dragging her heavy, wheeled bag behind her through the snow and contemplated finding a callbox to contact Greg and ask him to come and get her. It wasn't what she wanted to do, drag him away from the girls and Christine away from her family at this hour, but other than trying to find a hotel for the night on Christmas bloody Eve, she was running out of options.

She walked in the direction of the taxi parking area and as she got closer, she realised that the cab was still waiting at the kerb, and the man who had hailed it was walking away down the street. His black coat flapped around his legs. Scrunching her eyes, she watched his retreating form.

She arrived beside the cab as the man in the

distance turned again and raised his hand to wave. Her heart leapt in her chest. *But... he got off... I saw him get off...*

The driver's window was wound down, and she heard a voice from inside. "Hey, love. I'm guessing you need a ride. Where are you off to?" His broad Scottish accent was a welcome sound. Music to her ears and heart.

She bent so that she could speak directly to him. "I'm heading up to Clachan-Seil. Is that too far?"

"Not at all, love. I live at Knipoch, so it's not far from home. I wouldn't see you stranded on Christmas Eve. Well... it'll be Christmas morning, technically, when we get you home. Got to take it steady with the roads being icy." Mallory was familiar with Knipoch. It was a tiny hamlet of pretty houses on the shores of the stunning Loch Feochan, only around seven miles from Clachan-Seil. She felt a little better knowing the man wouldn't have too far to travel once she was home.

She looked down the road again, but there was no sign of the mysterious stranger from the train now. *Tiredness can do such silly things to a girl*, she thought, determined to explain away the impossible events of the evening.

Once she had opened the cab door, she climbed

in, pulling her bag in after her. "How come you're working so late on Christmas Eve?" she asked the man, feeling a twinge of pity that he wasn't at home with his family.

"I love to work Christmas. People are usually in really good spirits and keen to get home. I like to think of myself as a facilitator."

Huh? "What do you mean?"

"Well, you know. People only get a cab when they need to be somewhere fast. And so I like to think that I'm helping reunite families at this time of year."

She smiled. "Awww, that's really sweet. Are the roads really bad?"

He glanced at her through the rear-view mirror. "They're not great, but thankfully the gritter lorries have been out in force. The car's four-wheel drive, and if I take it steady, we should be fine."

She chewed on her lip for a moment. "But what about you getting home to your family so late at Christmas?" She could hear the concern in her own voice.

He laughed lightly. "Oh, don't worry, love. I'm used to this weather. I've driven in much worse. I'll be fine. I was just about to go home when something compelled me to stop and check for passengers. I'm glad I did."

Some*thing*, not some*one*. She gulped. "Y-yes... me too. Thank you."

As if sensing she wasn't really in the mood to talk, the driver didn't utter another word. Instead he turned up the radio and let the sultry sound of "Santa Baby" by Eartha Kitt fill the small space as he quickly typed something into his old-fashioned cell phone.

"Ahh. Dammit. Network's jammed or something. No signal. Mind you... I'm not surprised in this weather. I had a fare earlier who was having the same trouble. And he said the call-boxes he'd tried were down too. Who'd have thought it in this day and age?" The kindly man shook his head but didn't appear to expect an answer.

She played her conversation with the stranger on the train over and over in her mind. He seemed to *really* care. It was as if he didn't want her to miss out on life. But what was it to him? Why did he care? *Oh, come on, McBradden, you're being ridiculous... aren't you?*

He'd mentioned Monty Python... one of her favourite shows. He'd talked about her relationship with Greg as if he *knew* her. She remembered that he had asked her if she would have changed anything with Sam if she'd have known how things would turn out, and he'd seemed so happy when she said she wouldn't have.

She thought back to his face. His amber eyes with a hint of both green *and* brown. His shaggy hair... a similar style to Greg's but the colour of Sam's. The goatee. The familiar and comfortable feeling she'd had when talking to him and when he touched her briefly. It was as if she *knew* him. Her lip began to tremble as more of his words came back to her...

"And if, God forbid, you do lose him, you wear bright colours and celebrate the good times you shared." It was exactly what they had done for Sam... over in Canada. They had gathered and told their memories of him and released Chinese lanterns. It was as if he'd *known...* or he'd been watching.

His strange accent sprang to mind... a strange combination of Scottish and maybe American... or... or *Canadian?* More tears escaped her eyes and trailed down her face. *It can't have been him... he looked so... different... but the same too.*

Finally she remembered that he'd called her Mallory when she simply couldn't remember telling him her name. They had agreed on no specifics. She plainly remembered that. He had told her to *be happy*—a sentiment expressed to Josie in her dream as a message by someone with amber eyes. He had somehow got off the train in the Scottish Borders yet been able to hail her a cab in Oban.

She began to shake.

She had never believed in ghosts. Well, it wasn't that she didn't *believe* as such, but she was rather sceptical when it came to the supernatural. But now? Now she wasn't sure if she knew how she felt, or if there was some kind of logical explanation for this whole thing like she had said to Josie. Had she been dreaming? No... no, she would've known. She would've remembered waking up like every other time she'd dreamt of Sam or had a nightmare about losing Greg and the girls. Not this time though. It was all too... too real. He'd said he would be spending his time with his dad, reminiscing. Sam's dad had passed away too.

As the driver put the car into gear and prepared to pull away, she suddenly spoke. "Please, wait... sorry, can you just hang on a moment whilst I go and check on something?"

The driver swivelled in his seat. "Is everything alright, love? Have you forgotten something?"

"Erm... yes. I won't be a minute. I promise. I'm so sorry."

He applied the handbrake once again, and she climbed out of the cab. She began to walk down the road in the direction that she had seen him disappear. Her feet slipped and slid as she hurried through the snow. *There has to be an explanation. There has to be.* With tears streaming down her face and confusion fogging her brain, she trudged down the road as fresh snowflakes danced to earth around her.

She strained her eyes and peered into the distance, but there was no sign of the man. Not even a footprint in the snow. Realising she had walked a little further than she had intended, and with a heaviness in her heart, she turned and began to walk back toward the waiting taxi. She took a deep breath and turned around once more just in case he was there in the shadows.

But he wasn't.

Arriving back at the taxi, she brushed the snow from her hair and clothes, opened the door, and climbed inside.

The driver glanced at her through the rear-view mirror. "Did you find what you were looking for, love?"

Biting back a sob she replied, "No... no, sadly, I didn't."

"Well, you should call the station tomorrow. You never know. It may have been handed in."

She smiled and nodded as fresh tears sprang forth. Turning her face away, she stared into the distance as the cab began to whisk her towards home.

Was he an apparition? A ghost? Was he a dream or some kind of Christmas presence? She would probably never really know. The more she thought about him, the more she realised that he was, in fact, almost a perfect combination of the two loves of her life. Why *was* that? If it *was* Sam, why had he changed so much? Why did he resemble Greg in so many ways too? The beard, the shape of his eyes. The fact that the green had been replaced with amber.

As cottages decorated with coloured lights and then the farms and villages faded into snow-covered mountains and moorland, she was thankful that the roads had been cleared enough for them to make their way through toward home. Her mind whirred as she continued to replay the conversation she had experienced. What did it mean? If it was just a dream, was there more to it?

As she thought things through, yet another realisation dawned on her. The fact that the two men apparently had merged suggested that they were of *equal* importance in her life. Maybe that was what she was supposed to glean from this whole thing? *Both* men had impacted her life deeply and *both* were so very special to her. Sam somehow had led her to Greg, and she'd been so happy for so long—but she was on the verge of letting go, and for all the wrong reasons. The conversation on the train had made her realise just what she had and what she could've lost.

Mallory and the driver continued along the road in the treacherous conditions as the snowfall became heavier. She checked her watch, eager to get home. Greg would be beside himself with worry. Should she ask the driver to stop at the next call box maybe? She needed to let Greg know she was safe. She needed to tell him she loved him.

As the thoughts were whizzing around her mind at a hundred miles an hour, the driver suddenly jerked to one side and gripped the wheel, trying to straighten the vehicle. Mallory reached up and clung to the handgrip above her head as the car swerved left and then right. Her heart leapt into her mouth and she closed her eyes as hot tears sprang forth.

A string of expletives from the driver filled the

space in the cab and she heard a scream somewhere close by. She opened her eyes as the car spun in a circle and she realised the scream had come from her own body.

Images of Greg and Sam merged into one in her mind and she prayed for the car to stop safely. Words from her conversations with the stranger on the train came back to her in bits and pieces like a jigsaw, and she recalled the encounter in the shop and the sign he had pointed to. A voice filled her mind with the phrase, *"The past is past. Each day is a new beginning."* She didn't want to leave Greg like this. Not the way Sam had been taken from her. It just couldn't happen. She wanted her new beginning. Her chance to start over with Greg.

The car stopped suddenly, and the driver unclipped his seatbelt and climbed out of the car. He appeared at her door and tugged it open. "Are you alright, lassie? I'm so sorry. Black bloody ice. Are you okay?"

Mallory nodded, unable to speak, as tears of relief streamed down her face.

The driver reached out and squeezed her arm. "Thank the Lord someone was smiling down on us tonight, eh? Let's get you home."

fter over an hour of travelling from Oban in less-than-pleasant conditions, and a terrifying near death experience, the cab driver drove over the hump of the stone bridge, turned right down the lane, and came to a halt outside the little white-painted cottage that Mallory had grown to love. A string of multicoloured lanterns twinkled across the front of the property, and a lamp glowed behind the curtains in the living room. She could just make out the tiny footprints interspersed with man-size prints on the snow-covered garden. A little snowman stood in the middle with its parsnip nose and blue button eyes. His scarf was the bright blue Caley Thistle scarf that Greg was so fond of, and Mallory wondered how Mairi had convinced him that the snowman needed it more than he did. But then again, she was two and incredibly cute. The wonky construction was topped off with Mairi's pink *Peppa Pig* hat. It was sweet to see that Greg and the girls had been playing there. Her heart warmed.

Home at last.

She paid the driver and grabbed her bag. "Thank you so much for bringing me home. Please drive carefully. I'll worry about you."

He turned in his seat to face her and smiled warmly. "Like I said, love. I'm used to it. If it gets too bad out there, I'll get wrapped up and wait 'til morning. I've always got a couple of sleeping bags and a big warm coat in the trunk. Oh, and a nice flask of hot chocolate courtesy of my good lady wife. I'm not daft. I know when to call it a night. But it's not far to home. Only around seven miles, so please don't worry."

She thanked the kind man again and dragged her bag from the vehicle. He waved as he disappeared back across the bridge over the Atlantic, and she watched until his taillights winked out as the car descended the far side of the bridge. He was gone, along with the fears she'd been experiencing. It was as if the driver had taken that part of her baggage with him. She smiled as she realised. The door opened behind her and she turned around. Her breath caught in her throat.

Strong arms scooped her up and lifted her from the ground. "Oh, God, Mallory, sweetheart, I've been so worried." He carried her inside and kicked the door closed behind them.

She felt dampness against her face and pulled away to look into Greg's glistening eyes. Reaching to brush his cheek, she told him, "I'm home now."

His lip trembled as he stroked the hair away from her face and locked his intense gaze on hers. "I hope you know how much I love you, Mally. I hope you know what you mean to me." His voice broke, and she hated that she'd caused him to doubt her feelings for him.

"I do... I *do* know. And I'm so sorry."

Confusion clouded his ruggedly handsome face. "Sorry? For what?"

"For how I've been acting lately. I know I've been distant... distracted. And I'm truly sorry. That's all over now. I promise."

He shook his head and cupped her cheek in his large, calloused palm. "I was so scared that I was losing you. I don't know what I would've done if—"

She covered his hand with her own. "Greg, you aren't losing me... *ever*. I was scared too. I was scared

LISA HOBMAN

that everything would go wrong and that I'd lose *you* —like I lost Sam. Things are so wonderful, and I was terrified that it would all go wrong, but... something made me realise that I can't think like that. I *have* to live for now. I *have* to remain in the present with you and our girls. Worrying about what *might* happen or what *could* happen will get me nowhere. I understand that now."

He brushed the tears away from her cheeks with his rough thumbs. "What... what made you realise?"

"I think... I don't want you to hear this the wrong way, so let me finish. I—I think it was *Sam*." She was on the verge of explaining everything that had happened in Yorkshire and on the train journey home but stopped herself. It would be enough for her to explain the heart of the matter without delving into the whole thing about ghosts. "I think remembering *him* and thinking about *him* helped me to understand more than I ever did that *he* brought me to *you*." Her voice wavered as she gazed up into his chocolate-brown eyes. "That you and I were *meant* to be together. We've been through so much, and you're too important for me to let fear get the better of me and spoil what we have."

Tears trailed damp lines down his face, and he

huffed out a long shaking breath. "So you're *back* with me? You're *mine* again?"

She smiled through her own tears. "Oh, Greg, I've *always* been yours."

He returned her smile and closed his eyes for a moment, shaking his head. "You don't know how happy you've made me, sweetheart. Here's to the best Christmas ever." He crushed his lips into hers and took her breath away. She clung onto him as their tongues danced. She was home again; not only physically, but emotionally and metaphorically too.

Greg was her home.

Deep down she'd known that all along. But as her mysterious train companion had said, "*Fear can do strange things to you.*"

How right he was.

Lifting her from the ground once again, Greg shouldered open the door. He carried her up the stairs to their bedroom and placed her gently on the bed. She shrugged off her damp coat and tossed it to the floor. He stood before her with his penetrating gaze fixed on her and pulled off his T-shirt, exposing the muscled planes of his chest and abdomen. She hungrily took in the sight of his body, and desire spiked at the juncture of her thighs.

She could never tire of him.

Greg shed the rest of his clothing and crouched before her. He grasped the hem of her sweater, pulling it from her body in a gentle sweep. Next her jeans and panties were relinquished, and she eagerly unhooked her bra.

He lovingly met her eyes with his own and stroked her cheek. With a delicious, heart-melting smile, he told her, "You mean the world to me, Yorkshire girl. Don't ever forget that."

His use of the pet name so similar to the one she was used to hearing from Sam surprised her, but for some reason it didn't upset her. It simply made her smile, and that seemed to trigger something deep within him. He pushed her back into the billowing white duvet, climbing atop her and moulding into her like he was a missing puzzle piece that made her whole.

And he did.

She wrapped her legs around him and welcomed him into her body, closing her eyes as he kissed and caressed her breasts. Meeting his loving gaze with her own once again, she saw raw emotion, passion, and adoration reflected back at her.

Although it wasn't so long since they had made love, this felt different. She wondered if he felt it too.

As if reading her mind, he whispered, "It's so

good to have you back in my arms again. Where you belong." Gripping her hands in his as he rested his forehead on hers, he continued, "We belong together, Mally... forever."

"And we will be together, Greg. Always and forever."

The most amazing sensations rippled through her body as he moved inside of her. His features relaxed eventually, but his gaze remained fixed on her. He knew her. Every inch of her. And he worshipped every inch of her like she was the most precious thing he had ever held. His hot breath covered her face and neck as the saltwater from her eyes overflowed.

It was almost seven on Christmas morning when Mallory stepped outside the front door, wrapped in Greg's old fleece and her warm pyjamas. She had felt compelled to take in a few breaths of fresh, Scottish winter air. Even though she had been gone only a few days, it was as if she were breathing it for the first time all over again—seeing the place through fresh eyes somehow.

Peering out over the icy water, she remembered the first time she had stood on that very spot on the afternoon of the move to Scotland. Sam had been on his way, but tragedy had struck and he'd never made it. Instead her life had taken a whole new path. Josie had called Sam her guardian angel once, and now Mallory believed it to be true.

She opened her eyes and inhaled deeply once more. Movement in her peripheral vision caught her eye, and she turned to face the bridge over the Atlantic. Her breath caught as she thought she saw a familiar figure standing in the centre. She raised her hand and the figure on the bridge raised his hand too. He smiled and locked eyes with her for a moment before turning away. Closing her eyes, she shook her head to rouse herself from what felt like a daydream; and when she opened them again, Sam was gone.

The thing that surprised her the most was that the urge to chase him had gone too. A sense of contentment washed over her and she smiled.

"Merry Christmas, Sam. I'll never forget what you did for me," she whispered, her breath clouding before her.

Hearing the front door to the cottage open, she turned as Greg appeared in the doorway. "Hey, sweetheart are you coming in? Mairi'll be awake soon and I think our hungry little Sylvie is ready for breakfast."

Mallory smiled at the ruggedly handsome man before her. His ruffled dark hair was swept back from his forehead, but strands had fallen forward. His melted-chocolate-brown eyes were filled with love, as always, and his smile made her heart skip. He wore a tatty old A Perfect Circle T-shirt that once was black but had faded long ago to grey. His bare feet poked out from beneath his tartan pyjama pants, and he hugged his muscular arms around his body.

He stepped toward her and she held her hands out. "Whoa, stop! You've got nothing on your feet! It's freezing out here."

Ignoring her protests, he completed the short walk to reach her and encircled her in his embrace. "Is it? I can't really feel it when you're wrapped in my arms." He placed a gentle kiss on her lips and rubbed his nose down the length of hers. "Come on inside. I've opened a bottle of Buck's Fizz. Let's go get our girls and make some Christmas memories, eh?"

She nodded and lifted her hand to run it through his silky, soft hair. Pulling herself up on her tiptoes, she took his mouth in a kiss that she hoped would express just how she felt for him. That the connection they had went way beyond lust... far beyond love. They were soulmates—inextricably linked to one another for all eternity.

She would never doubt that again.

And ironically... it was all thanks to the man she had once thought she was destined to be with forever. It was all because *that* man had given her the best Christmas gift she could've hoped for.

Sam had given her the strength to look forward without fear.

EPILOGUE

Five years later

Christmas morning

"Daddy! Get up! He's been!" Greg opened his eyes to find two very lively, dark-haired little girls bouncing on the bed.

He yawned and stretched. Reaching out briefly, he stroked the empty pillow to his right. Peering up at his bright-eyed daughters, he tugged them down into a bear hug. "Oh. No, I think I will just stay in bed all day and catch up on my rest." Closing his eyes, he feigned sleep and pretended to snore, but the girls weren't giving up without a fight.

"Daddy," Mairi commanded.

"Yes, come on, Daddy." Sylvie lifted his arm and waved it around like a rag doll, determined to get his full attention.

Greg sat up and huffed. "Okay, okay. I give in. Go on downstairs and I'll be with you in a minute." When the girls still sat there, stock still, looking expectantly at him, he lifted his hands and wiggled his fingers. "You'd better go, or the tickle monster might attack." That did the trick, and the girls squealed before dashing off the bed and down the stairs.

He pulled on his lounge pants and an old faded T-shirt and went to the bathroom. The reflection in the mirror looked like it needed more sleep, and when he walked back to the bedroom and glanced at the bedside clock, he discovered the reason.

It was six o'clock.

Awww, fudge. He chuckled to himself, shaking his head, and walked toward the stairs. As he approached the living room, he paused to listen to the giggles and rustles of paper coupled with the sound of "When Santa Got Stuck up the Chimney" playing in the background. His heart swelled.

He quietly stepped around the door into the room and took in the scene before him. Mairi and

Sylvie sat there sharing the brightly wrapped gifts into piles.

"This one's for you, Mairi, but this big one with the shiny pink bow is mine." Sylvie's sweet little voice melted his heart. She was five and a half going on twenty-five, that one. Quite bossy for such a young girl.

Mairi rolled her eyes. "Well, I've got a big one too. Just you wait and see when I open mine." She might as well have accompanied her words with *neener, neener*.

Both girls turned at once and spotted him standing in the doorway. "Come on, Daddy! Come on!"

He made his way over and plonked himself down on the floor beside the smallest pile of gifts. "I'm guessing these are mine, then, eh?"

"Well, Daddy, you are a growed-up, so you can't have as many presents 'cause it wouldn't be fair if you gotted more than us," Sylvie informed him. A wide grin spread across his face.

As he sat there, he felt a shiver down his spine and turned. There standing in the doorway was the most beautiful woman he had ever seen. Her face lit up with a heart-melting smile as she gazed lovingly down at him.

"Good morning, handsome."

Clambering to his feet, his walked over and cupped her cheek in his hand. "Good morning, gorgeous. Wow... you really do get more beautiful each day."

She blushed and reached up on her tiptoes to kiss his lips. "Flattery will get you nowhere, Mr. McBradden," she told him in a husky whisper.

"Oh, I sincerely hope you're wrong." He glanced at the little bundle in her arms. "And who is this fine fellow?" he asked playfully.

"Daddy, you know who that is, silly," Mairi called from where she sat in front of the tree.

Greg scrunched his brow, and Mairi and Sylvie giggled. "Nope... nope, never seen him before in my life."

"Daddy, you're such a big silly. That's baby Sam."

Greg wagged his finger and grinned. "Ooooh, I remember now. He's the one who makes quite a lot of mess and noise and wakes us up at two o'clock in the morning."

Mallory rolled her eyes and joined in with the giggles. "Yes, and *someone* didn't wake up this morning even though it was *his* turn," she chastised.

"Hey, I needed my beauty sleep," Greg protested.

Mallory laughed, and the sound warmed him. "Come on. Let's get this show on the road." She kissed Greg once again and made her way to the floor to join the girls. She placed baby Sam in his bouncy chair. His scruffy dark hair stuck out at all angles as he chewed on his fist.

"Can we build a snowman later, Daddy?" Sylvie asked, clapping her hands.

"Oooh, yes," Mairi chimed in, "but it has to be bigger than the last one. Angus peed on it and made it go all yellow." She shivered. "Eeeeugh! And then Ruby dug a big hole in it."

Mallory and Greg burst into laughter, and Greg ruffled the dark curls of his older daughter's head. "Angus and Ruby are getting on a bit, sweetie pie. We'll not let them near the next one, eh?"

Sylvie folded her arms and huffed. "I want to open my presents now."

Mairi began to pass the gifts out, and Sylvie began to rip the paper off with fervour. Shreds of red, green, and gold confetti fluttered around and fell to the rug as Frank Sinatra sang "Have Yourself a Merry Little Christmas."

Greg slipped his arm around his wife and kissed

the side of her head. He gazed down at the sleeping baby boy where he lay in his chair next to Mallory. *Baby Sam.* It was only right that he was given that name, just as Mairi had been given the name of the woman Greg had loved before Mallory. Mairi and Sam had been the two people who inadvertently gave Mallory and Greg the common ground to build their relationship from. And looking at his family there before him, all smiles and giggles as they discovered what Santa had brought for them, he decided he was the luckiest man on earth. It had been a rocky road to get there, but so many years on, he was deeper in love than he ever could've imagined. And Mallory had given him the best gifts he had ever received, better even than their three beautiful children.

An unlimited supply of unconditional love.

The End

ACKNOWLEDGMENTS

To my best friend and husband, Rich, I would be lost without you. To my beautiful daughter, thank you for letting everyone know how proud you are of your mum and for wanting to follow in my footsteps.

Mum and Dad, your unconditional love keeps me going through the times when I doubt my abilities. Thank you so much.

Huge hugs to all my friends for being there and for encouraging me to take time away from my laptop.

To the numerous blogs who have supported me, let me take over their pages and have shared my teasers and book details. You seriously rock!

ABOUT THE AUTHOR

Lisa was born in Yorkshire, England. Her passion for writing began at a young age when she started to pen stories and poetry whilst at school. Nowadays she can be found tapping away at her laptop almost full time. When she takes a break from writing she spends time looking after her daughter and husband or walking her two canine companions.

After relocating with her family to Southern Scotland in 2012 she began to write her Scotland based debut novel, Bridge Over the Atlantic (published 2013). In 2014 the novel was shortlisted in the Contemporary Romance category of the Romantic Novelists Association RoNAs. This meant a trip to London for an awards ceremony where she had the opportunity to meet her favourite authors—some of whom were also shortlisted in the same category.

Three years after beginning her writing career in earnest Lisa now has a total of ten contemporary romance novels published—several of which have become bestsellers on Amazon, iTunes and Barnes & Noble—and three erotic romances under the pen name Lissa Jay. Her erotic debut, Bad Company also hit the bestselling eBook charts in the USA and the UK on Amazon and iTunes.

Being a crafty and creative person, Lisa spends any spare time singing in a trio with a guitarist and drummer or making book related items to give away to her readers via her Facebook page.

ALSO BY LISA HOBMAN

Printed in Great Britain
by Amazon

32984312R00108